APOLOGIA

Spineless Wonders
ABN98156041888
PO Box 220 STRAWBERRY HILLS
New South Wales, Australia, 2012
www.shortaustralianstories.com.au

First published by Spineless Wonders 2020

Typeset in Adobe Garamond Pro

National Library of Australia
Apologia /Michalia Arathimos
1st ed.
ISBN 978-1-925052-64-0
A823.4

A catalogue record for this book is available from the National Library of Australia

This project has been assisted by the Copyright Agency Cultural Fund.

APOLOGIA

MICHALIA ARATHIMOS

Contents

The Beauty of Mrs Lim

Mrs Lim was so small she could fit in Mrs Maniakis's pocket, Mrs Maniakis said. Her eyes were black like cold hard beads and her eyebrows had been plucked and drawn on, so she looked like a movie star, she said. Mrs Lim was like one of those little China dolls you could get from China, where she was from, like a little souvenir, Mrs Maniakis said.

'God, Mum,' her son, Peter said. 'Can you even hear yourself?'

Mrs Maniakis was concerned that Peter might have misunderstood.

'She was beautiful,' she said. 'Beautiful. Like a little agalmátio, a figurine.'

'You're being problematic, Yiayia,' her granddaughter said. 'You can't say she looks like a China doll, not anymore.'

'She doesn't know she's being problematic, poor thing,' Peter said, and patted Mrs Maniakis's hand.

'I don't have any problemata,' Mrs Maniakis said. 'I'm saying she was a koukla, like a little toy. You're the one with problemata. The Devil's going to get you.'

She swatted Peter's head with a tea towel. Her grand-daughter laughed.

'But seriously, Yiayia. You can't say that,' she said.

'You don't understand,' Mrs Maniakis said. 'This Mrs Lim, we loved each other. She loved me. I loved her for years.'

Peter gave her a strange look. She went on drying the dishes.

The invitation for Peter's end-of-school prize-giving came in a thick white envelope with gold-embossed lettering. Mrs Maniakis could read it: they had been in New Zealand for more than ten years and she had taught herself to read and write. The only English book in the house was the dictionary her husband read at night after he got home from the fish shop. She didn't read that – the letters were too small. But she read the ads for groceries in the newspapers, and she read the signs at the shops. It was surprising how many English words she recognised, once she had learned the odd, naked-looking alphabeto.

'It's almost like they borrowed some of the words,' she said to her husband. Her husband raised his eyebrows one after the other, individually.

'Agape mou, they did,' he said. He gave her a familiar look, the one that said that she was small, and precious, and to be protected. 'They took a lot from us; the language, democracia, philosophia. You didn't know?'

Mrs Maniakis smiled.

'No, Stavro,' she said. It was a game they played, but she really hadn't known. She had left school when she was eight years old. Stavros laughed. Everyone laughed at Mrs Maniakis. She was small, and she was easily flustered, and she made silly mistakes. Sometimes she thought Stavros had married her so he would have something to laugh at, like a monkey in a cage. But he treated her well. He bought her things. He never raised his hand.

She ran her hands along the fine paper of the invitation. They were to go in dinner wear. She would have to have her black dress dry-cleaned. She hoped her leather pumps would be sufficient. There were some more words at the bottom:

Ladies, a Plate

She waited for Peter to get home to ask him what this meant.

'It means you have to bring something to eat, Mum,' he said. 'You have to bring a plate of food to share.' Her son's face went slightly pink.

When they sent him to school he couldn't speak English. He often came home with welts on his legs. Mrs Maniakis couldn't understand how not knowing something was a caneable offence, but his teachers knew what was good for him. He learned the language quickly enough, though he would always hate school. Early on he had asked her to stop putting feta in his lunchbox, to leave out the olives, to please send him with something more *normal*.

'Don't worry,' she said. 'I'll do something Anglasika, for the prize-giving. I'll make an English dish. Scones, maybe.'

'You mean those pieces of flavourless dough you're always going on about?' Peter asked. But he grinned as he walked out of the kitchen.

There's just something about her,' Mrs Maniakis said to the ladies at the church group. 'Usually they're so quiet, the Chinese I mean. But this one, she's strong. She's different. She doesn't care what people think.'

'If we didn't care what other people thought of us, how well do you think we'd do in this country?' her friend said.

'They'd throw us out.'

'They'd send us back.'

'They like us because we don't make trouble,' her friend said.

She was right, Mrs Maniakis thought. Stavros's boss said he liked to employ Greek people. They were quiet, and hard-working, he said. He said they were alright.

'Mrs Lim doesn't make trouble,' Mrs Maniakis said. 'She stands very straight. Like a lady. Like a Chinese princess.'

'Look at you,' one of the ladies said. 'Anyone would think you were in love.' The chorus of voices rose, their laughter tinkling around Mrs Maniakis.

Mrs Maniakis looked into her coffee grounds. Her mother used to read them. All she could see was a dark mess, with a kind of jagged shape at the edge, like a wound.

When Stavros had first come into her she had cried out in pain. Then it got better for a while, but then, after the children, worse. There had been a problem. She would never look, of course, but now there was a smooth place as if she had been burned. She kept quiet when he did it. He was a good man, and it was always over quickly.

'Poor little thing,' her friend said. She touched Mrs Maniakis's hair. 'You shut up, all of you!' she said to the chorus of laughing women. 'Don't you know the smart bird is grabbed by the nose?' She looked at Mrs Maniakis closely.

Mrs Maniakis looked deeply into her cup.

The day of the prize-giving ceremony, Mrs Maniakis wore her good shoes, the newly dry-cleaned black dress, and her most expensive scarf over her hair. She took her son, uncomfortable in his long pants, and her husband in his best jacket, and, most importantly, a pavlova. She had followed the recipe exactly. She had never seen a pavlova, but the strawberries against the white of its surface were pretty.

After the ceremony, the parents milled about in the school hall. Mrs Maniakis approached the table. She saw there not only her pavlova, but two others: fine, high things crested with hard crusts and cream. Now it was clear to her. Among the lamingtons and the ginger slices and the custard tarts, her pavlova was a sad, slumped thing, a failed imitation. The other parents avoided her pavlova in favour of the others.

Peter messed around with his friends near the back. There was a boy close to them, an Asian boy, talking to no-one. He was also called Peter. Mrs Maniakis had asked who he was once, when she had accompanied her Peter to school. Nobody, Peter had said. She had asked where who his friends were. No-one, Peter said. He hardly says anything to anyone.

Stavros circulated, making small talk. She lingered near the table. There was one other untouched dish, a plate of translucent steaming bundles.

She saw the woman suddenly. Like her, the woman hovered near the table. She had fine posture, blue fine lines instead of eyebrows, a delicate face, coiffed hair. There was something stubborn about her, you could see it at a glance. It was the way that she stood, the way she was closed off to conversation. She was shorter than Mrs Maniakis herself.

A couple of women passed up Mrs Maniakis's pavlova in favour of the scones. One of them looked at the bundles curiously. They didn't whisper or laugh. But, as they settled on the bench, they looked again at that plate, and then at the woman standing next to them.

Mrs Maniakis advanced upon the plate, and took one of the bundles. In her mouth, it burst with unexpected depths of flavour. The pastry was soft and smooth.

'Stavro!' she called. 'Peter!' Her voice rose above the parents' heads. 'You must come and taste these!'

Peter ignored her. Stavros came over and took one of the bundles. She took three of them, four, five, many more than was polite. The two women's eyes widened. She jammed them into her mouth. She turned to the upright woman, who had been watching her all the while.

'Delicious!' Mrs Maniakis said, with her mouth full of food, as loudly as she could.

Mrs Lim smiled.

The day she was invited to Mrs Lim's, Mrs Maniakis woke with a feverish feeling. She did her hair carefully and then redid it, even though it would be concealed under her scarf. She wet her eyebrows and smoothed them. She put on the tiniest bit of lipstick: the one Stavros had got her when they'd married.

Mrs Lim's house was like theirs – small and wooden with a neat front yard. Inside there were photographs along the hallway, with odd things decorating them, red and gold things. Mrs Maniakis didn't look too closely at these, or at the dragon sculpture in the living room.

'My husband,' Mrs Lim said, waving at one of the pictures. 'Dead, now. A long time.' She looked Mrs

Maniakis in the eye, and crooked her mouth up at one corner, as if to say, 'What can you do?'

They drank green tea, which Mrs Maniakis found unaccountably strange. She ate a kind of white sweet cake. Then Mrs Lim brought her into the kitchen, where she taught Mrs Maniakis to fold dumplings.

'Very fine, her work, very fine and quick!' Mrs Maniakis said to Stavros, later. 'You should have seen her hands! They were flying!'

Stavros laughed at her. He laughed the second time she went too, and the third. But then the women at the church began to talk. It was a small neighborhood. Everyone knew everything.

'I think you should stop seeing Mrs Lim,' he said one day.

'You have burned my nerves,' Mrs Maniakis said. 'May the priest turn on your lights.' Then she saw that he was serious.

'It's best that you stop seeing her now, before it gets worse,' Stavros said.

A hot red thing went up and down Mrs Maniakis' body. The hot red thing stayed in her, and it had no escape.

In the village where she grew up, Mrs Maniakis had seen many things. They kept dead bodies in houses in those days, even in the heat of summer. They killed their own chickens, their own goats. When the war came, the people in the cities had no food, and they came to their family's door, begging. Her family only had dandelion greens, and olives, and a little flour. Sometimes their mother would give the beggars something, if it was a woman with a child. More often, they kept their food for themselves.

The worst thing she saw was what happened to the girl who'd had a baby without being married. The father of the child never came forward. The Italians came. The Germans came. One night, the girl disappeared. She had been given to the soldiers, the villagers said. Some time later she was found near the edges of the village, a motionless heap.

Mrs Maniakis was still very young, but she went with the others to look. Some of the boys threw stones. The girl's blood was crusted across her face. There was blood on her skirt, and her clothes were torn. She had been there a while, and she stank.

They didn't bury her in the churchyard, because she was a sinner.

Peter was in his twenties when he came home with the news. Mrs Lim's son, Peter, had been killed. It wasn't certain what had happened. People were visiting the house.

The next day Mrs Maniakis set out for Mrs Lim's. There were many cars outside. Mrs Lim opened the door.

There was a young woman behind Mrs Lim. Mrs Maniakis handed her the koliva, the dish she had made in commemoration.

'You came,' Mrs Lim said.

Then she was against Mrs Maniakis's chest, and Mrs Maniakis was pushing her into the house and closing the door, and Mrs Lim was holding her, her thin arms around Mrs Maniakis's waist. The daughter's eyebrows shot straight up on her forehead. Mrs Lim's hair was now cut in a short, sleek bob that ended under her chin. Mrs Maniakis felt it graze her cheek.

In the living room beyond was the babble of voices in Mrs Lim's language. The daughter tried to guide her mother and Mrs Maniakis there. But Mrs Maniakis offered her dish. Mrs Lim looked at the small mountain of icing sugar. She took the smallest pinch.

'Delicious,' she said. Her face was grey under her powder. 'What they're saying isn't true,' she said. 'Someone killed him. Peter.'

'Mum!' the daughter said. 'There were pills,' she said to Mrs Maniakis. 'They found pills on him. But Mum thinks someone broke in.' All of a sudden her eyes clouded over; she had not meant to say this much.

In the Greek church a suicide would not be buried with an Orthodox funeral.

'If Mrs Lim says Peter was killed,' Mrs Maniakis said, 'he was killed.'

There followed a strange sequence of events, a sequence Mrs Maniakis often returned to in memory, because she could never quite believe that it had happened. Mrs Lim whispered to her that she couldn't bear it, that she couldn't go back into the lounge, where her people were gathered. She pushed her daughter away. She led Mrs Maniakis to a back room, a dark room, and shut the door.

There, Mrs Maniakis started a lamentation, a formal wailing that women in the village would perform at a death. She hadn't known she was capable of it. She hadn't known that she would do it. Mrs Lim sat with her hands folded in her lap. She did not cry. Mrs Maniakis sobbed it all out for her: the boys who had bullied Peter at school, the way Peter had receded from Mrs Lim, the feeling of his soft, velvet head against Mrs Lim's chest when he was newly born.

Many people came to the door and tried to intervene. But Mrs Lim whispered to Mrs Maniakis, and Mrs Maniakis used her loudest voice to make them go away. This went on all that day, and through the night.

The next day, Stavros arrived. She heard his voice at the door, uncertain, then angry. He came into the room.

'I will come home tonight, Stavro,' Mrs Maniakis said. They never spoke of it again.

Many years later, Peter was at her house putting away the groceries when the phone rang.

'Yes,' he said. 'I see.' He hung up the phone. 'It's Mrs Lim, Mum. Mrs Lim, that Chinese lady you were friends with, remember? I'm sorry, Mum.'

Some time went by. Then she could hear Peter's voice again. The carpet was yellow and marmalade-patterned and next to her face, and she was on her knees. Peter was trying to get her to stand up. But she had been watching the small brown hands working, folding dumplings, so agile, so precise.

Mrs Maniakis worked out the complex route to the cemetery – a bus, a shuttle, all taking hours, ending at the high green space overlooking the sea, where Stavros and most of her friends were now. But Mrs Lim would not be buried, like Mrs Maniakis would be. Instead, her body would be transmuted, would be disappeared. Was already disappeared.

When Mrs Maniakis arrived, there were only a couple of people left at the headstone. One of these looked at her and walked away – the daughter, in her fifties now. The last seemed to wait.

Mrs Maniakis had brought a white lily. The woman took it. She was younger than Mrs Lim was when they'd met. The hair was the same, the shape of the cheek. Not the eyes. The eyes were blue. She took Mrs Maniakis in, with her black mourning clothes, the gold cross around her neck.

Would Mrs Lim go to the place where unchristened babies went? Or would she go to her own place? Would that place and Mrs Maniakis's overlap?

'You're Mrs Maniakis,' the girl said.

Mrs Maniakis nodded. She was looking at the grass and at the high rocks around them. Mrs Lim's body was nothing now – ash. Had they scattered what was left of her? Was she in the air?

'She always talked about you. You should have heard her, like you were the best of friends. But we never saw you.'

'They didn't let us,' Mrs Maniakis said.

The girl had a ring through her nose and stood sloppily, like a boy. Then the girl stepped forwards and embraced her, a full body embrace, her head under Mrs Maniakis's chin. For a moment, her hair was Mrs Lim's hair. Mrs Maniakis felt gravity go weird and wrong. Then the girl stepped back, and it was over.

'My grandmother always said she loved you,' the girl said. She waited, as though Mrs Maniakis might have something to say. Mrs Maniakis looked at the blank stones.

'I'm sorry for your loss,' the girl said.

Mrs Maniakis should be saying this to her, the granddaughter, not the other way around. What was she playing at?

But two hands, folding dumplings.

'Thank you,' Mrs Maniakis said quietly. Then again, 'Thank you.' The last time she spoke in a clear voice, and her voice went out and rang against the stones, and went up into the air. 'Thank you,' she said, in her loudest voice, the voice that Mrs Lim had loved.

The Highway Woman

If her city was like a heart it was cleft into two chambers, each distinct and velvet-red, left ventricle and right, split down the middle by Elizabeth Street, with Flinders Station the grand aorta. Magda knew most would probably mark the dividing line as Swanston Street, with its fine, high-ceilinged library, its Town Hall, and the vicious cathedral rearing up at the end, as if, she thought, to clout the being it was gesturing towards. But Elizabeth Street was the street she knew best in the city. That was where Magda went when she had money to burn.

She wouldn't burn it today, though. She had an orderly list involving undergarments and a hat, a winter coat and the special wooden apparatus. She would not be diverted. But the smell of roasting peanuts, cinnamon, honey, a thick caramel signature, and the clip of the horses' hooves and the air itself, thick with sooty undertones that she read, coming in as she did from the suburbs, as evidence of things happening – movement, progress, the ambulant residue of industry, and the grime set in layers that could be deciphered archeologically, washing up from the street she walked on and along the rough-hewn sandstone walls, like sediment lines in cliffs near the sea, and the gold trim of the post of the penny arcade she was passing, her feet striking the cobbles in excited syncopation in her second-best shoes, a little worn now but chosen for their comfort (a small heel, modest, real leather, navy blue, with a buckle, still serviceable), the rush and jingle of it, the city, with a tram now rattling past her, its red and gold marking it out like a soldier on patrol, carrying workers in their hats and coats to a hundred destinations, and what affection she had for it as it rumbled along (she caught one every day, along Sydney Road before alighting at Brunswick), and the din of it filled her and threw her so she hardly knew herself, and the shops just now opening, for she'd timed it so she would beat the crowds, and here she was more than just herself, she was greater, breathing the caliginous air as easily as the businessman beside her or the couple further ahead, the girl with her hair done in curls, her waist nipped in enviably – after having her son, Lou, Magda had found it hard to feel the same, and now she caught a reflection of her body in the window she was passing, itself a tableau of cashmere scarves whose colours gave her pause, for one was a peacock blue, plainly tropical, and she'd not seen anyone wearing such a fist of blue like a sock to the eyeball, it must be something new they were bringing in this year, perhaps she could pull it off, but for a moment she'd seen herself: a middle-aged woman, baggy-faced, thickened at the waist, the bust bolstered up, the hair, despite her ministrations this morning, flattened at the top, *fallen* – and for a moment all the colours passed out of her and it was not her city after all, the couple now moving quickly on ahead, the businessman clipping onwards to something important, another tram shouting past with workers hanging off the sides, even this man prone at her feet begging for alms felt suddenly distant, his face twisted and a hat on the ground empty of all but an old bronze penny, as if the passers-by had forgotten what a boom they were in the midst of, and in fact, at work, Magda had noticed a slight downturn in the generosity of her clients, a creeping stinginess, as if the fields had ceased raining gold, the men fingering the sovereigns before they lay them down, and now a horse and trap, traversing the great vein she walked upon, passing out of her still, the clop of the horses with their plumed heads leaving her untouched, for she was a bag lady in the mirror, this finished thing, this creature in whom femininity was stalled, used up, halted, the ankles too thick (the plate glass extended all along the side of the department store, imported from England, they said, it mirrored and mirrored and would not let up), and beside her reflected a lady with smelling salts, her kerchief held to her nose in defence against the stench, and now Magda smelled it, the sulphurous reek of the gutter, the slops or whatever had been tipped into it by those hand-to-mouth families that lived in holes along Little Lonsdale Street, and against the image of the lady (young, corseted, small boots, fine wrists), here she was, her figure blurred as if her outline had been filled with deadening sand, *We walked the sands of Williamstown, my darling, my darling, we shall never be apart*, a figure so coarse and used to the scent of the city that she had not thought to shield her mouth, and she was finished, she could scream, tear her hair, burst into pieces here in the middle of Elizabeth Street and no-one would notice, she could rend her garments, but the businessman would keep walking, though the man with the girl might turn, and briefly, the girl's face might show compassion, and the lady with the kerchief would lean on the arm of her beau, and be whisked away from the sight of her, Magda, on the ground, but now one of the horses (dressed in finery that was red and grey) neighed and tossed its head, and Magda shook herself at the shoulders as if she was being shaken by another, and felt her toes in her shoes, her real, second-best pair of shoes, on the real cobbles of the real street, and she would not let herself waste time being captured in the glass.

The sound reminded her:

Tlot-tlot; tlot-tlot! *Had they heard it? The horsehoofs ringing clear;*

Tlot-tlot; tlot-tlot, *in the distance? Were they deaf that they did not hear?*

— but the smell of roasted peanuts, and the city itself, they took her and they drew her, and she was entirely diverted.

Lou had brought the poem home from school and had been memorising it to help him learn his letters. *The Highwayman.* Magda could not read beyond spelling out the bills that came each month from the landlord and sounding words out one letter at a time. At the schoolhouse in Scotland, with the potbelly fire in the corner and the cold slate pressed against the lobe of her hand, she'd tried. But the letters moved and switched around. When she wrote d, Schoolmarm said it was a b. The cane didn't help her focus, neither.

Now, turning to the peanut vendor beside her, preparing to bisect the aorta and traverse the crowd at the bottom of Elizabeth Street, aiming for the station, the lines ran through her mind again: *Tlot-tlot; tlot-tlot!* An odd poem to give to an eight-year-old, she'd thought. Bess, the landlord's black-eyed daughter, was in love with a highwayman. Then King George's men came marching to her inn. Bess knew her love would be riding down the road to see her. She knew they'd shoot him on sight. They caught her, the Red Coats, and bound her to the foot of her bed. They fixed a musket underneath onto Bess's chest, pointing to her heart. Then they kissed her.

Magda had tensed at that. But Lou put his hands behind his back cheerfully and stood each night to attention, in front of their small open fireplace. The words tripped off his tongue.

The peanut vendor tried to cheat her but she knew the price of a scoop of nuts should be a ha'penny and no more. The brown paper crumpled in her fist. She felt tears start in her eyes, and turned away. An everyday subterfuge! Why should it bother her? She hurried in front of a horse and nearly got run over at the end of the street. She ground the nuts between her teeth. The station's many clocks reminded her of the world, which she'd seen so little of. No bother. If her job had taught her anything, it was that men were the same everywhere.

The milliner's was the best, the one under the station. Already there were three in line ahead, proper ladies. They looked her over and took a quarter of a second to understand her. But she had the coin.

A burgundy felt, with white lace trim.

She glanced at the cathedral as if at an old acquaintance. It declined to nod. They both knew they'd never been close friends. Magda took Lou every Sunday to the Uniting, which sounded like an equivocal kind of name. Swanston Street now, for the coat, which cost more than expected, due to the wool exports. It wasn't what you'd get in Europe, but still: a warm camel, with small stitching, fine patterned lining. She ran her hand over it, wrapped in tissue in a carry bag, which she would keep.

Poor Bess! Waiting and waiting for her lover!

He did not come in the dawning. He did not come at noon;
And out of the tawny sunset, before the rise of the moon...

Get out of there, Bess, Magda would have told her. Save yourself, before it's too late.

The maker of the wooden apparatus was in Chinatown, among the hanging ducks. She went down a staircase and was ushered into the underground workshop. There she chose from an array of harnesses and fittings. Size was a concern – too big, and she risked losing customers, too small, and it would be comical

– but she liked the idea of big, which was malicious. There was a part of everyone that wanted to punish, as much as there was a part that wanted punishment. She settled on a medium, allowed the craftsman to show her how to attach it, and slapped his hand away.

The title of Lou's book was *A Treasury of Children's Verse*. She would sit near him and watch as his small hand, still chubby, traced the letters.

They said no word to the landlord.
They drank his ale instead.
But they gagged his daughter, and bound her,
to the foot of her narrow bed.

She supposed this was what the teachers chose to keep the children interested. Half of them would leave school young. Some worked evenings and fell asleep with their heads dipping into their inkwells, Lou had told her. He'd shaken his head in a worldly way, and said it couldn't be helped.

Lou, though. Lou was to be a doctor, if it killed her.

There was the sound of the horses again along Swanston Street, in the air that seemed clean after the fug of the workshop. She'd traversed the edge of the aorta and moved into the left ventricle. A cell moving, that was all she was, an organic unit in transit.

Lou had inherited an illustrated anatomy book, not from his father, who had made his entire contribution to his son's life efficiently, briefly, standing up, behind the pub where Magda worked, but his stepfather, Thomas.

Who was gone as well. *My darling.*

Magda liked to pore over the book, imagining Lou would someday use it. *Aorta. Ventricle.* Spelling out the words, letter by letter. Thomas had taught her anatomy. He liked to say he'd given her a broad anatomical understanding. He would only ever say such a thing in private. He was respectful, but full of mirth, his eyes crinkling up at the corners.

Lou's father had been the first. When she found herself with child, she'd thought at least she hadn't a family to disappoint. The nuns whispered, and the shopgirls, and the pub girls, and Magda had needed to stop work for a while. But as she said to Mary, the woman who taught her the trade, who was Magda? Magda was a person, it turned out, who didn't give a flying toss what they all thought. They'd have taken her son away from her at the hospital, so she didn't go to hospital. *A fallen woman.* She vanished. And kept Lou.

Thomas hadn't appeared to mind her lack of husband, or hear the Scottish in her voice, neither. But she fuddled the names on the list at the waiting room at his surgery. He'd drawn her aside two days into it. She was to be his Nurse Assistant. He needed a steady hand to pass the implements and old Daisy shook and flailed at amputations and the like. Did she think, if Daisy took over at reception, she might be willing to learn?

Thomas was a ship's doctor, temporarily moored. They married a year later, on the wharf at Williamstown. *We shall never be apart.* Lou was there, with his red cheeks. He was meant to be carrying a thistle to signify Scotland, but at the last moment one couldn't be found.

> *There was death at every window;*
> *And hell at one dark window;*
> *For Bess could see, through her casement,*
> *the road that he would ride.*

Magda had eaten her cinnamon-flavoured nuts. They left a sickly taste in her mouth. She bought raspberry jawbreakers for Lou at the last moment. She caught the Sydney Road tram, her hand resting on the felt of her new hat. Clothes were money in the bank. But nothing was quite like money, except money. Money would proof you against death. They said this was the richest city in the world. The streets were paved with money. But once there had been no streets. Once, there had been people with another language here, a much older language. The tram pulled past the Royal Park.

Home was a haven with coal to be lit and potatoes to boil. She placed the apparatus in the centre of the table. She would move it before Lou came home. The wooden shape was curved becomingly.

She'd not have believed she could find the work interesting. When she'd begun, a year after Thomas's death, having moved from Williamstown, *My darling, never be apart*, it was good to work. The money was better than she'd get from the factories or the mills. And Lou could go to school in the city.

The days were a litany of strange bodies. She was good at it. She became better. She became sought after. Now and then she would come to herself, hand on an arm or a leg, moving inexplicably, masterfully. She was a specialist; men came to her to be handled, to be made to do things, to relinquish power. She used a wooden tool and made herself manlike. Sometimes she felt powerful, but it was a lot more like being a mother than she'd expected. The same need to provide care.

A year after their marriage, Thomas had been called to sea. A month after that, a letter. No body, no details. An accident, at night. A seafaring man's wife took her chances. Everyone knew that.

Aorta. Ventricle. We walked the sands of Williamstown. My darling, my darling.

When he was courting her he would throw stones up at her window, and she would hear his voice singing a local song badly. Even from the street, even with his voice lowered so her landlady would not hear, she could pick up the edge of humour. *Never be apart.* As if it was their private joke, the idea of always being together. As if he thought she believed in forever.

The one thing she didn't like about her work was that the fleshiness of it had begun to supplant her real memories of him. Thomas's back, moving under her hands.

By the time Lou stood to recite to her, after dinner, Magda was settled, her back in the narrow wooden chair, a spud in her belly, black tea on the table between them. Lou's face, fair and freckled, and his red hair, looked nothing like hers. His eyes were a pale blue, like Thomas's. He reminded her of Thomas, not of his father, but that was just wishful thinking. As if she had wished Thomas into his eyes, when they were really someone else's.

Poor Bess! She was still waiting for her highwayman, with a musket bound to her breast. But she writhed and struggled, until one finger touched the trigger. Lou swayed slightly as he chanted the words, a thin invocation.

Tlot-tlot; tlot-tlot, *in the distance.*
Were they deaf that they did not hear?

Lou's eyes began to fill. He gulped the tears back. Bess watched for her love in the moonlight. When she heard him, she shot herself, warning him with her death. Lou was determined not to cry. Magda pulled him close and held his small body against her chest. The fire crackled.

He stepped back, stood tall again, and pushed his way through the end of it. The highwayman heard what Bess had done, galloped after the troops in a rage, and was shot down himself on the road.

Blood red were his spurs in the golden noon;
wine-red was his velvet coat.

Lou sat down and put his head abruptly on the table.

Magda's heart beat. Lou still had to feel all of it, see it: all the wine-red velvet of it, all the ventricles, all the passages, all the seascapes and streets and traps and hats and industries, all the wenches and wretches, *all the never be aparts*, all the other-languaged buried underneath or forsaken, all the gold, all the *My darlings*.

'Why did they have to die, after all that, Ma?' he asked.

What was she to tell him?

'It's just the way of things,' Magda said.

The teachers had been right to give him this poem, after all. She gave him a raspberry jawbreaker, from the bag, and took one for herself, biting down on the hard sweetness.

If her heart was like a city it was cleft into two parts, one strawberry-red, one cool and pale, left ventricle and right, split down the middle by Lou's birth, with Thomas the grand aorta, and herself, a cell in transit. Thomas was carrying her, still, and she would do her work, and when all the rushing about was done she would come to rest in the right place, sleeping, finally, crimson, vivid, useful, *a part*.

*All quotes are from 'The Highwayman' by Alfred Noyes, in
A Treasury of Children's Verse

An Appropriate Response

Pete and Nicky Rose were in Byron Bay for the summer. Pete was a bit of a punk. He showed it in the animal welfare patches on his cut-off jeans, in his short, hacked hair, and in the ring through his eyebrow. He was considering taking the eyebrow piercing out: it was getting too mainstream. Nicky Rose was a big, lush, messy-looking girl, a girl who wore bright red lipstick as a matter of course, and purposely blurred it round the edges of her mouth.

It was one of those summer days that generously stretches out, burning on and refusing to leave the party. The river curved out of town and hazed off into farmland, cradling bush around it. It was midsummer, and the campers were scattered through the bush, calling to each other, laughing, cooking food. Nicky Rose and Pete were walking down the river with their packs, singing. Nicky Rose was wearing a leopard-print coat, despite the heat. Pete was carrying a marrow.

'I'll tell me ma when I get home the boys won't leave the girls alone,' Nicky sang. 'Old Irish lullaby,' she said to Pete. They were nearing a bend in the path, and she sang louder, her voice going ahead of them into the air.

'I like your singing, usually,' Pete said. 'But can you just, well, it's not that I don't like it and everything, but...'

Nicky threw her head back and laughed. 'You're not trashing my Irish roots, are you?'

Pete shifted the marrow in his arms. It was huge. He'd been carrying it since they'd left town and his hands were starting to sweat. Pete was a vegan. He came from good, solid stock in Queensland; his family had also been miners and, more recently, loggers, all, firmly, of the meat-and-three-veg persuasion. This veganism was a new development and started when Pete had renounced his father's values and taken a stand, locking himself on to a tree in the forest his father's company was about to fell. His father's colonisation of the forest mirrored his lack of respect for the animal world, Pete felt, and besides, steak gave you heart disease. But sometimes, like now, with the faint smells of other people's barbecues wafting fulsomely into his nose, Pete felt his veganism as a hard choice, an injustice, and an inconvenience besides. And so, he was forced to carry this organic marrow, which had seemed a good idea in the fruit shop in town, but which now slumbered greedily in his arms like a great, fleshy creature, lazy and hideously benign.

'I would never trash someone's cultural roots,' Pete said.

Under the trees, the sun dappled the ground. Its gentle appearance belied its searing heat. Pete couldn't believe Nicky was wearing that fake leopard-skin coat. They'd argued earlier about how it wasn't real fur but still looked like it was. It was a matter of choosing to function within a repressive paradigm or outside of it, he'd said. She'd argued for free expression and won.

'When the wind and the rain and the hail blow high,' Nicky sang, 'and the snow comes shovelling from the sky.'

In front of them was a waterhole. There was a tyre floating in the middle with three guys floating on it, smoking. There was an older woman at the edge of the water building a papier-mâché duck. There were some cute girls, sunbathing. There was a family having a barbecue. The smell of meat was infiltrating the air. Pete looked down at the marrow. It was hard work, being vegan.

'Look,' he said to Nicky. 'I just don't get it. It's hot and sunny and you're wearing that coat and singing about rain and hail.'

Nicky studied him, in his Docs and skinny jeans. He was overdressed, too. Then she shook herself dramatically, in her fake fur. The bells on her pack jingled.

'Are you telling me my singing's not good?' she asked. 'Or is this really an Irish thing? It is, isn't it? You think you're better than me?'

She was dangerous. There was no telling when Nicky Rose was really angry. He and Nicky didn't know each other that well. They were more summer acquaintances, friends of friends. Pete could feel in her a deep bubbling hilarity that both attracted and repelled him. In the fruit shop she had flirted outrageously with the boy behind the counter and sung lewd songs to the apples. When she got to the bananas, Pete had hurried her out, afraid to see what she might do next.

'It's not that your singing's bad,' Pete whispered. 'Hi,' he said. 'Hey.' They were passing the two bikinied girls. 'How's it going? Yeah,' he whispered to Nicky. 'It's just that it might not be such an appropriate response to the scene.' He gestured broadly at the sun, the bathers, holding the marrow aloft as a pointer. They rounded a curve in the path and moved into a quieter stretch, where the river narrowed and sped on and the banks rose up, dense with greenery, the water inaccessible.

'She's as sweet as apple pie, and she'll get her own man by and by,' Nicky sang.

Further down, the river arced out of the sweet bush and into an open stretch of grass. They were both hot and sticky by now, scratched, jumpy, a little electric. They'd been stomping and laughing next to each other on the dusty path, him in his boots and she in her sandals. Nicky was still singing Irish tunes.

Ahead of them the path petered out into a clearing by a wire fence. They were brought up short against the mesh. Beyond the fence, the green stretched wide and unnaturally perfect. There was no way forward.

'It's a golf course!' Pete said. He pressed his hands on the wire. Beyond it the green had an unreal, food-like quality. The grass looked almost edible. 'I can't believe it,' he said. 'This used to be parkland. They must have bought it from the council. Must have put it in last year.'

Nicky had stopped singing. She looked deflated. Suddenly, she threw her pack on the dirt and grabbed Pete's arm.

'Brother,' she said, passionately, 'brother. This is what it's all about right here! Can't you see? It's a test!' Her eyes were dilated, the pupils wide and black.

Pete looked at her and back at the green, dazed. It was a different world in there, the manicured lawn, the little poles with flags, the horribly trimmed trees. Then he remembered something.

'Wait!' he said. 'Where's the marrow?'

'It's okay, Pete, it's okay, man,' Nicky said. 'It's right here.' She showed him the marrow strapped to her pack on the ground, sitting across the top like a bedroll. Pete passed a hand across his eyes. That was right, Nicky had offered to carry the marrow a few river bends back. Nicky Rose was back at the fence; she was pulling off her coat.

'It's time, man,' Nicky said. 'It's time to act. Can't you feel it?'

She threw her coat onto the ground. She pulled off her singlet and she pulled off her bra. She stood in front of him in her smooth skin.

'You coming or not?' she said.

Pete tried not to look at Nicky – he tried not to look. But there she was in front of him: round, beautiful, complete – not at all like the cringing girls at school, so scared of their bodies. Not like Pete himself who, pulling up his shirt now, in front of Nicky's bold gaze, had to fight not to pull it straight down again. Next to her he felt skinny, pale, altogether inadequate. But she caught his eye. He was amazed to see she was beaming, openly appraising his half-bared chest as if frankly inspecting a piece of fine art. Under her eyes it was impossible to feel ashamed. Pete pulled off his shirt in one movement and unbuckled his belt.

It was hard to get over the fence. It was hard for Pete especially. He kept looking back at the marrow, all soft and helpless on Nicky's pack. It looked so vulnerable, like a newborn baby. Maybe he shouldn't leave it.

Nicky was over already. She looked at him as he balanced precariously, one foot on either side of the barbed wire.

'The marrow will be fine,' she said. 'It's just going to chill there, okay? It can fend for itself.' She threw her head back again and did her wild laugh.

Pete jumped down, landed wrong on his ankle. Then he was face down on the grass, on the fresh clean new grass, and it was caressing him softly. It seemed horrific that he'd never played like this in the sun before, never let the grass and the earth touch his skin – a terrible travesty.

'Privatise this!' Nicky was screaming. Pete saw her cartwheel away down the green, her tan-lines stark, her skin brown and white like a patterned bird.

Seeing the group of golfers was like seeing something out of an eighties movie. Their chequered red pants were creased down the middle, their socks were white, their shirts funny pastel yellows and beiges and blues. They were all rotund. They wore visors. Nicky Rose and Pete were hidden in the bushes, watching them. The golfers moved across the land like football figurines, as if on grooves. One hit a golf ball and it soared away; two others raised their hands against the sun.

'That's a beauty, Rob,' one of them called.

'That's it,' whispered Nicky. 'I can't handle it! I can't handle any more! We have to show them.' Her eyes were keen and bright. She was panting a little in her flushed skin and it was a surprise to him to realise again their lack of clothing.

'Nicky Rose,' Pete whispered. 'What…'

'An appropriate response!' said Nicky Rose. A smile edged its way around her mouth.

Before he could hold her back, she'd stepped out of the bushes.

She lifted her head and tossed her ponytail. She grinned at him and ran away down the green, towards the golfers. One looked up.

Pete stepped out, felt the sun on his skin.

'What the…' he heard one of the golfers say, as Nicky ran towards them, sprinting, wobbling gorgeously.

Pete ran. He whooshed down the slope towards the little men. He caught up with Nicky, grabbed her hand, and they flew together around them, around the men's astonished faces. They ran a circle around them, and the men stood with their chequered bags on wheels and their clubs and their white shoes. The men's gasps were audible as they swooped around again, laughing now, panting. Nicky cried out.

'Like what you see?' she called, and Pete understood suddenly that it was different for a woman. 'Like it? What am I to you?' she screamed. 'A dancing pony? A show pony!' She broke free of Pete and leaped alone into the sun. She threw back her head and neighed, braying loud into the rough. She neighed again. She trotted in tighter and tighter circles round the golfers, screaming with laughter, clapping her hands, her white teeth flashing in the sun.

Pete had never seen anything so beautiful.

He took a breath. He looked around at the perfect, wonderland green, the men in little golfing suits, the emptiness of the fenced-in land, the grass like icing on a cake. Back at his pack, the marrow waited, vulnerable, unguarded. But he was with Nicky now.

He began to prance.

Nicky Rose's response was to act like a show pony, and Nicky Rose was hugely and unalterably right.

Bearing Witness

A grapefruit, black coffee, email correspondence. I tidy for the clients, but at this time of the morning my papers are sprawled across my desk. The referral form from the court says she's sixteen. I usually find my youths are too young to be cognisant of the consequences of their choices. Already I suspect she had a background of disadvantage, peppered with calls to the authorities, unexpected relocations in the night. There are the offences, laid out like an easily solvable puzzle: theft, obstruction, robbery, a pattern of escalation. She's on the verge of crisis. One more offence and she'll end up in the correctional facility, and then, later, jail. It's up to me. I sense she has no-one else.

By the time we have our first appointment I consider myself prepared. I've read up on the incidents. I've studied her background. I have an informed picture in my mind: the mother gone, the stepfather at home and employed at the meatworks, younger siblings deposited with various other relatives. I think I'm ready for her.

She walks into my office, a tall, sloped thing, twenty minutes late. She's beautiful, but she doesn't think so. She's got the kind of 'fuck you' energy that easily gives way to tears. I make her coffee (milk, two sugars). Her voice is faint, as if she's speaking through a scarf.

I tell her that it would be normal to go through some post-traumatic stress, in her particular case. I tell her I'm here to help.

This is how the girl looks. She has a tattoo on her forearm of a dragon. She has a ring through her nose. Her eyebrows are thick and full, and she has a broad mouth, with a slight dark fuzz over her top lip. She wears no makeup. She has a black top on, loose jeans, sneakers. The girl has bloodshot eyes. Her hair is scraped back off her face and wrapped around itself into a knot on top of her head. It's pulled back with absolute precision, each hair gelled into place.

She takes the coffee. She seems to be studying something behind my head. She doesn't bring the cup to her lips. The quiet reaches out and I wait through it, like they taught me to wait, counting, so as not to speak. Wait time, it's called. When you think it's finally time to say something, wait a little longer.

But still she says nothing. Her eyes are fixed on the wall.

I go through my mental checklist for signs of drug use. Some of them are there. I'm not meant to admit it, but sometimes, I believe escape is an appropriate response.

I ask about the police, about whether she thinks they've treated her fairly. I ask her about solitary confinement in the facility she's being kept in. She answers my questions reedily, her voice a stone skipping over water. Her expression grows bemused. I get nothing out of her. Platitudes.

At the end of the session I escort her into the waiting room. I have learned superficial details: she went to an all-girls school, she likes art and music, and she wants to be a dancer – hip-hop or fafswag (I shall have to look this up).

She doesn't hold herself like a dancer. She holds herself like someone is going to approach her from behind with a knife. I want to put my hands on her shoulders. I want to tell her that her life will improve.

On her way out, she speaks so loudly that I jump.

'Why don't you just ask me?' she says. 'I know what you want to ask. What's my big secret? Why did I go off the rails?'

'You're my priority,' I tell her. 'I do want to know, everything, but you can tell me in your own time.'

I don't wear political T-shirts anymore. My hair is cut into a sensible bob. I'm wearing a scarf from a boutique down the road. I retired my ripped stockings long ago. How do I make her understand that I'm on her side?

I put my hand on her arm, my fingers pale against the curved tattoo. She flinches. O Theos, Maria. So stupid. She looks at me with enmity, as if she's going to hit me, or run.

Sometimes I still think in Greek. When Greeks are upset, they say someone has 'broken their nerves'. I have broken the girl's nerves.

She laughs.

'Nah, I get it now,' she says. 'You don't want to just figure out what led me into all this. You're the type that wants to save me.'

Many of my clients push back against me in place of something else.

'This isn't about me,' I say. 'This is about you.' I make my voice sincere. I make my face neutral. I allow myself a hint of a smile, for reassurance.

The girl's mouth lifts, slightly, on one side.

'You talk a good game, lady,' she says.

There's another old Greek saying. Translated literally it means: 'The many words are poor'. In English we might say something more like this: 'Talk is cheap'.

Adam looks good. I try not to dislike him for it. He goes to the gym often, maintaining himself and managing to look impeccable like some men do far into their middle years. I myself do not look this good, though we are of a similar age. Too many glasses of red wine and too much agape for my native Greek cuisine.

He asks after Liesl, who has gone back to Germany for a brief sabbatical.

'It's good, you know, it's all good. Space is healthy.'

Adam gives me his signature look, the one where his left eye trembles slightly, almost out of sync with the right.

'I feel like I'm rediscovering parts of myself I haven't been in touch with for years.' My voice is rising. The parts I'm discovering are those that watch reality television and comfort-eat after dinner, the parts that can down whole blocks of chocolate in one sitting. Liesl loves chocolate, but she is never excessive.

'If you insist, sure. Space can be a healthy thing.'

I ask after Sebastian.

'His work is going well. It's very demanding, by all accounts.' He steeples his fingers. 'You're diverting.'

'I'm genuinely interested.'

Adam has been my supervisor for ten years. I ask about Adam's life with Sebastian because he is my friend but also because I am trying to figure out what keeps them so apparently content. There is no greater mystery than other people's happiness.

'Yes, but this is about you,' Adam says. 'It's the girl, isn't it? You're fixating.'

'Not like that, if that's what you mean. Not at all.'

'I'm not accusing you of anything untoward. But it's clear the case has upset you.'

'I wouldn't say I'm upset. She keeps running out on me, that's all. We'll be ten minutes into a session and she'll storm out. I'm just not getting anywhere with her.'

Adam rolls his eyes. 'All progress is illusory. We don't want to subscribe to some flawed ideal of a linear progression from "sick" to "well". The reality is you probably won't be getting anywhere with her, not really. Not in ten sessions. People have catharses and plateaus, and sometimes regressions. That was why you wanted to work with me, remember? Because I think the current models are too simplistic. We both know that when you tick the box at the end, she's not going to be cured.'

'But we do have to believe, don't we…'

'That what?'

'That we can effect some change? Even just by being there. By bearing witness.' Adam takes a sip of wine. 'Believe whatever you have to believe, Maria.'

In the next session, I ask the girl about the police, about what they did to her when she was caught. She wasn't taken quietly. She resisted.

'Is there a time in your life you might like to talk about, a time you felt out of control?'

There had been some violence. She had made a complaint. It was never followed up. She'd had no advocate for a while, something about her caseworker changing jobs. The complaint was somewhere on someone's desk, waiting to be filed.

She yells at me this time, before walking out.

'Jesus,' she says. 'What do you know about my life?'

I know how oppression works, I could have said. I know the impact shame has on the body. I know what it is to suffer.

But maybe after all she's right; maybe I don't understand.

This time Adam came to me. I'm on my own leather couch, in my office. I'm lying on it, my feet in their stockings pointing upwards gracelessly.

'Bearing witness is an interesting concept, isn't it? Like you're carrying something. Or enduring it.'

I am too tired for this. All I need is for him to tell me how to keep her here, how to pin her to this couch, so I can talk to her at least.

'But the observer is distanced from the subject by the very act of performing the observation.' Adam studied Jungian psychoanalysis in Europe. He did his thesis in France – something about parapraxis and Lacan.

'You're being pretentious, Adam.'

'I trust you to keep me on my toes, darling. So you're bearing witness. So what?'

'She's not even close to letting me do that. She just thinks I'm a stuck-up, middle-class bitch with a salvation complex.'

He fixes me again with his look, the trembling eye.

'Maybe you are.'

And suddenly I'm standing, my face flushed, my body propelling me towards the door.

He knows me, my migrant background, all my complex history. I have never needed to walk out on Adam. But if I stay, I'll cry. I don't want to cry over this. Then Adam laughs.

'Maybe we both are,' he says. 'Stuck up, middle-class bitches, I mean.' He looks at me until I bend, sweating, and lower myself back onto the couch, putting my face in my hands. He considers me. 'It's the end of my workday. Let's go and get a glass of wine.'

'Very unprofessional of you.'

'I know a place up the road that does a great Merlot. Oaky, rounded and rich, with almond overtones. Definitely a stuck-up vintage.'

And I'm laughing, even though I know maybe he's right. When did I become middle-class?

It's when we leave the room, arm in arm, that it strikes me. He had made me, for a moment, into her.

My father hit us. It didn't hurt me much, because it was impersonal. To him, and to my mother, it was expected. His ownership of me was an inalienable fact. It was there in the way that you spelled my name. Maria Antionopulou, not Antionopolus. The 'lou' was the feminine form. It meant I was 'of the' Antinopoluses: I belonged to them.

If my father hit me for stealing his cigarettes, for going out late, for taking his ouzo, it was merely a consequence of my actions. It was a linguistic impossibility when I was growing up, being female and Greek and not being owned. My father cared for his property.

Greasy Greek, greasy Greek, go back where you came from. She's a wog.

But I came from here.

I went to university and found out certain things. The world was hierarchical, the world was structured, the world was gendered and split. There were abusers, and then there were the abused. I went to protests and I was seized and I threw things. I cut my hair and dressed all in black.

I stopped going home. Everyone told me I had made the right decision.

When I met Liesl we were in our twenties. She was camped out in a sleeping bag at the edge of some contested Indigenous land, fresh off a plane from Germany.

'Are you part Indigenous?' she asked me. Her blond hair blew into her eyes.

'I'm Greek,' I said, afraid to disappoint her. But Liesl was not disappointed. She looked me up and down.

I found I was open to a range of possibilities. She was a bird here, looking down with interest. She decided, for a while, to alight. I was here but I was not fully here. Maybe that was what my father was trying to do, with each blow of his hand. He was trying to hammer me down, to adequately place me. He was trying to push my edges back, so I resembled a good Greek girl. *You have broken my nerves, Maria.* Sorry, Baba, I would say. *The many words are poor, Maria. The many words are poor.*

All these years later, Liesl is gone. The girl looks past me with her red, watery eyes. I lied. I'm a liar. It did hurt.

Adam and I have made an unspoken agreement to hold our sessions in a place where we can drink.

'He's good, Maria, Sebastian's always good.'

'But how? How are you both so good?' I'm too many glasses into the evening to be asking lightly.

He shakes his head. 'The girl's bringing out a lot in you, Maria.'

'Adam, I'm fifty-five. I have actually considered my issues before.'

'We are always taken surprise by what we think we have dealt with.'

'She's not some symbolic player in my life.'

Adam takes a sip of wine. 'Let's reverse it, then. If you were just a player in her life, what would you say to her? What change would you wish to effect?'

I look at the high colour in his face, and his eyes, which are swimming a little.

'You're drunk, Adam. Go home.'

Liesl calls from Germany. It appears she wants to stay on, for good.

'What does this mean for you?' Adam asks. 'Is it a break-up?'

'I'm not sure,' I say. I have already cried into the chardonnay. I have to give credit to Adam. At no point at the restaurant while the snot worked its way down my face did he give way to embarrassment. Not even when the waiter was tangibly concerned. Adam just waved him away and handed me a tissue.

'Well, if Liesl says she's there for an unspecified amount of time…'

'I guess it's over.' It's the first time I've really admitted it. I've been telling myself its temporary, even as I drafted the 'Flatmates Wanted' ad. I can't afford the house on my own. 'I'm going to have to get someone in. I mean, she might come back but…'

'She might not,' Adam says. He pats my hand.

'I mean, what am I going to put on the ad?' I say. My voice is two octaves away from a wail. 'Washed-up lesbian seeks similarly depressed single?'

'Whatever you do, don't forget to make it inclusive!' Adam says.

'Intersectional feminist, queer and vegetarian friendly, transgender welcome?' I say.

'So you're intersectional now?' Adam says.

'I'm intersectional by virtue of who I am, Adam.'

'I thought we were just tired second-wave feminists, at odds with the modern world.'

'You can't be a proper feminist, Adam. You're a man.'

He pouts at me.

'I can be whatever I damn well please, honey.'

What do I dream about, lady? I dream I have enough cash to get a hamburger at McDonald's,' the girl says.

I feel my face slump. Is she seriously requesting money? I look at her. She looks hopeful. Something rises up in me: a memory, me, myself, in a short skirt and school shoes, swindling some boy out of a cigarette. Taking it behind the back wall of the school and laughing. The girl reads my face, seems to give up.

'I dream of lasers,' the girl says. 'I dream I'm flying and I'm shooting lasers out of my eyes. I'm shooting them all down, the cops.'

I shake my head.

'When you're ready to tell me something serious,' I say, and I hear the prissiness in my own voice, 'feel free. I'll be right here.'

If I'm not wrong, she looks briefly devastated, before the cool indifference descends again, across her face.

'You think you see but you don't see anything, lady. You're like a branch that's been cut off, lying on the ground.'

'What?' the word has gasped itself out of me before I can stop it.

'I see,' the girl says. 'I see everything.'

Definite drug use, I write in her file. *Delusions of a spiritual nature.* And then I go home and eat chocolate and cry.

When we bought the house, it was a typical cottage in a run-down area. Liesl and I stripped the seventies wallpaper in each room, shedding layer upon layer from the walls. We had a transistor radio that only played two stations and the only paint we could afford was all off-tints, cheap tins left over from other people's mix jobs, so our house ended up painted in oranges and yellows and with the odd blue wall. The night we finished, we got a six-pack of beer and lay together on the hardwood floor among the scraps of old carpet.

That was before we got the workmen in to polish the floors, before I persuaded her to invest in a new marble bench top. The kitchen remodel came later, and the bathroom. Maybe it was the state-of-the-art stove or the kitchen sink with the invisible taps that did it. With each new modification I had to convince her to draw down more money on the mortgage, persuade her that it would all work out the same in the long run.

I remember wanting to show my father the beautiful house. But he died just when I had finished laying the beautiful bathroom tiles. He never would have agreed to meet Liesl anyway. He never saw what I had made, all the good work I had done.

You think when they die they will go away, that it will all go away. You think it will be easier to let it go.

Liesl's mad blue eyes in her sunburned face, that summer we renovated. The blue and orange paint striating her arms. The way she held my hips down on the floor, as if she would grind an impression of herself into me, as if her impression would stay inside me, forever.

It's the last session. I have failed.

Adam would tell me not to interpret the experience in this way. We do not have failures, he had taught me. We have continuums. We have processes. We have progressions and relapses and shifts.

We have a whole lot of bullshit. There's that old Greek saying: *The many words are poor.* I have done nothing for the girl. She has not even told me her story.

We run through the usual closing process. I talk about how her time here has concluded, how I hope that some healing has occurred. I wish I could tell her further help will be available, but it won't be. The state-funded counselling is finished.

She sips coffee out of her paper cup. She looks through me. All of a sudden, I'm done with pretending.

'What the police did to you was wrong,' I say. 'They shouldn't have seized you and searched you like that. And what your family did to you, that was wrong too.' I'm making assumptions now, I'm reading into it, I'm breaking all the rules. 'I want to tell you something: it was nothing to do with you. It was their violence, and you were caught up in it, nothing more. You were the victim of something that wasn't your fault.'

She looks at me as if she has just woken up. The fury in my voice is barely under control. Adam would tell me to back out now, to abort. But then, maybe he wouldn't.

'It shouldn't have happened,' I say. I shake my head. 'What they did to you. It makes me sick.' Now she is looking straight at me. 'I wish I could go back,' I say. 'I wish I could do something to make them stop.' I hear my voice tremble. I am gripping the edge of my desk.

She smiles a strange smile.

'When we hunt, the animal we catch is just the one that happens to be there,' she says. She leans forward, places the coffee cup on my desk. 'Nature doesn't care if the animal is nice or not, if it did anything wrong.'

She stands to leave. Her skin, her black hair, her tattoo, her colours in the small white room are blinding. She's almost crackling. She walks towards the door. Then something in the way she's standing changes.

'When are you going to learn, Maria?' she asks.

She's never before used my name. I didn't know she knew it.

'Why do you never listen, Maria?' Now her voice is rhythmic, like a series of blows. 'You have broken my nerves, Maria. When are you just going to let it go?'

She opens the door. Before she closes it, she looks at me again. This time her voice is almost gentle.

'I see you, lady,' she says.

When I tell Adam, that night, I am still shaking.

'What do you think she meant?' I ask. I need his counsel on this. I need this more than I ever have – to know what he believes. 'What do you think it means? It was him, Adam. It was exactly what he used to say.'

Adam pauses. He steeples his fingers. He gives me his characteristic thoughtful look, his left eye wobbling minutely. He hums one note and looks at the ceiling. He leans his chin on his hands.

'Maria,' he says. 'What the fuck do you think it means?'

Three Days, Two Apsaras, One Gold Ring

They are gentle with each other.

The marriage proposal has happened and they treat each other like cut glass; they treat each other like there's something in the air cupped between them that might break. In the tuk-tuk he looks over at her hair that's frizzled and vague with the heat and touches it. On the dirt lane by the backpackers hotel, she snakes an arm behind his back, pulling him away from a dark gutter. They hold hands as if willing each other to be solid objects. Everywhere they go people tell them they're beautiful.

They find a temple in the jungle, eaten through by trees and overgrown with vines. They wander in its cool, collapsed halls for hours. They see few others. He wanders off to take photos of fallen buildings and hewn stone. She loses him.

'Jim!' she calls. There are echoes. 'Jim!' She remembers what the guidebook said about the landmines, about not going off the path. The hot still air folds around her. There is the faint vegetable sound of the jungle breathing, of life too small to see. A dense quiet. 'Jim!' She starts to run.

She finds him in a clearing, bent over a rough stone. He's tracing letters on its worn surface. She grabs his shoulder, seeing the sweat darkening his shirt, his hair poking out under his green cap. His eyes are a mad hazel in his tanned face.

'Robyn, look!' he says. 'An Apsara, a dancing goddess.'

She breathes out fast, too winded to speak.

'This must be The Hall of the Dancing Apsaras,' he says, looking down, away from her, at the guidebook. The camera is at his side. He looks up. 'What's wrong?'

There's an embrace that starts with her sinking to her knees, in that stone place. Him touching her hair, dropping the guidebook in the white heat of the court-yard, them leaning together in the baking sun despite their need for a shower and a drink of water and his damp shirt and her ruined hair and just leaning in, the smell of them in this hot place together. She has her hand on the warm part at the back of his neck, she's flushed and dusty and her eyes are too bright, but it doesn't matter, not any of it, not this moment.

They stay that way till they hear the tour bus arrive.

Afterwards, they will find they've taken hundreds of photos of nothing, light falling across a rock, a root snaking through a wall, two feet disembodied on a pillar.

The second day they get hungry in the hotel room and go out into the street.

The street is something else. There's traffic and a wonderful tooting of horns, as if each bike passing is a celebration. But the street has people who try to touch them as they walk, Jim and Robyn, arms around each other, their money belts under their clothes. Robyn stumbles into a pothole and the liquid oozes around her foot into her sandal, surprisingly warm, the temperature of blood.

At the food stall it's mostly smiling that gets them the sandwich, as they have very few words. The baguette is filled with sharp, spicy leaves and chilli.

'Cheese you want? Cambodia cheese?' the lady asks. She's big, heavy, sulky with tourists. Robyn and Jim look at it.

'Not like foreigner cheese,' the lady says. She brings it out from behind the glass and waves it under Jim's nose. 'You not like?'

Jim bends and inhales dramatically, then leaps back in affected shock. Robyn can smell the cheese from where she stands. It doesn't smell like cheese at all. It smells like off fish. Jim waves his arms in front of his nose like he's trying to clear out the smell and the lady screams with laughter.

'You try?' the lady asks. 'You try, you like?' she gestures with the cheese at Jim again. Jim has his hands to his throat now and everybody's laughing. Robyn looks at him, thinking who would have guessed when we were at home, thinking something about how you find out about people, you really find out, when there's no language, as he mimes choking, beaming wildly, on the hot street.

Suddenly, hands grip Robyn's. She jumps. They're hot and dry and thin and small. She backs off, trying to pull her hands free, but there's a little boy still grabbing at them. He's tiny, the size of an eight-year-old, but his face looks much older in the half-light, his head too big for his body.

'Madame, please, Madame,' he says, holding her hands.

Robyn's breath catches in her throat. Next to her, Jim turns, sensing her step back onto the perilous road. The motorcycles bleat and roar.

'Madame, I am hungry, Madame,' the boy says. She can't speak, it's like she's choking on dust. 'Madame.' The boy's voice turns to a sob and he's there, unbelievably against her now, gripping the cloth of her T-shirt in his hands and twisting into it, his body pressing against hers, his arms tight around her waist. A motorcycle toots and swerves. She's raising her hands, but not pushing him off. He's small and she doesn't want to hurt him. There are cracks around his mouth filled with dust and his dark eyes, looking up, and his smell.

'Get off!' Jim is there and pulling at the boy, taking the little dry heat against her chest and flinging it away. The stall lady's voice is rising in a shriek. 'Come on,' Jim says to Robyn.

'Check your money belt,' he says, a few steps down the road, in a low voice. She does, but nothing's gone.

'I didn't know what to do,' Robyn says. 'You're not meant to give them money, we decided that, didn't we, Jim? Not to give them money?'

Jim doesn't answer.

'The thing is,' Robyn says thoughtfully, 'I don't think he was putting on an act at all.'

The third day, they go to the royal baths. The sun blares down. A fountain stands crumbling in the centre of a stagnant pool, green and furzed with heat. Jim takes photos of Robyn. Robyn is in the business of looking. She pays particular attention to the stone elephants' trunks, the dragon with three eyes, the lion spouting water from its open mouth.

By the time they come back to the hotel, Robyn has a headache. The traffic squawks in through the window like the sound of fighting gulls. Jim wants to go out for dinner. It's the kind of day where she looks at him as if he is the enemy, as if he is the problem they are trying not to see – the beggars waiting on the streets, the children with maimed hands and legs lying in wait for tourists.

'Just go without me,' Robyn says.

Jim kneels on the bed, takes her hands, kisses her.

'Please come,' he says, eyes wide. 'Robyn. Please come with me.'

They go to a fancy place near the centre of town. It has actual menus, in English and Khmer. It has waiters. They never could have afforded it at home. They sit in their loose green travel pants and sandals. Robyn wears a red singlet. Her skin blushes under the fairy lights strung along the lane. She's brushed out her blond hair; it's curling around her face. Jim has her favourite green T-shirt on. There are wooden beads at his wrist, a greenstone at his throat. The waiter comes and goes. People pass, selling photocopied guidebooks, Angkor trinkets, T-shirts. They ignore them politely.

The first course comes and it's fish, with a papaya salad on the side. They look out at the fairy lights in the lane, the quaint dirt footpath. Robyn picks up her fork with a little clink. The little clink is new. It makes her look, see again the bright new gold on her finger, the engagement ring.

'More wine?' Jim is on his best behaviour. He pours her wine and she sips too fast, choking on the tannin at the back of her throat. She can't stop coughing.

'Robyn! I'll get some water.' Jim gets up.

As soon as he's gone the coughing stops.

'Here, darling, here.' Jim has come with water and she looks at him quietly, not coughing. It's funny. She feels the joke of it rise up to her face. They laugh. Jim sits down.

'Who would have thought we'd be here?' Robyn asks. Suddenly, it's all so easy, her body in the chair, her throat relaxed after the choking, the warm air. 'I mean, who would have thought we'd come this far?' An old man rides past on a bike, bells jingling, a baguette in a paper bag on his back.

'I know.' Jim's face opens out at her and she feels spoiled to have him look at her like this, like she's the only thing in the world.

They are holding hands under the table when the man comes.

'Sir, Madame, please to give me something,' the man says. 'Please to give me something for this pretty-pretty, this dancing Apsara.'

In the moment before they look at him, they look into each other's eyes. They are so close in this moment that it almost hurts. They both know they shouldn't turn, that to speak to him would be false encouragement. But he's standing there, waiting. Robyn will later remember Jim's hand in hers under the table, his eyes bright in his face. How they knew exactly what the other was thinking. How they tried not to see.

They look at the man in the same second. He has no hands. He is waving his stumps at them, roughly rounded stumps, healed over like nothing, like nothing in the world but arms with no hands. Over one stump hangs an Apsara charm, dancing on a chain.

The man doesn't say anything. He doesn't repeat the offer. He stands, truncated arms held up, smiling broadly, as if he'd made a joke.

'I, we, we're sorry,' Jim says over his rich fish sauce, the remains of their salad.

'No, thank you,' says Robyn firmly. 'No, thank you.'

She looks at the fish. It seems suddenly congealed, revolting. The man is grinning now, waving. As they try to look elsewhere, he laughs out loud, advances towards their table.

Robyn looks at Jim. He's getting that look he gets.

The man is laughing louder, stepping forward. Robyn flinches. In two steps he will be touching her face.

'Hey, just wait a minute.' Jim is on his feet in front of the man, his hand clenched into a fist.

Robyn will say afterwards that she didn't know what she was doing. She had no money in her pockets, Jim had the money belt, she didn't have any change of her own. Her only thought was to make the man go away, to get him safely away from Jim.

Robyn stands and snatches the Apsara from the man's arm. His stump brushes her skin. It's soft, boneless. She thinks of sudden force, a jolt, a landmine going off in the jungle. Heat and blood.

But where to put the payment? Jim's hand is still raised but he doesn't move as Robyn steps firmly forward, as she places the gold ring delicately, gently even, into the man's mouth.

The man walks away, laughing through his teeth.

In the empty street, on the dirt path, beside their lukewarm meal, Jim takes her hand.

'I thought we had agreed,' he says. 'Not to give them anything. I thought we were in agreement.' He looks at her naked finger. That's when she knows. She knows it will stay naked.

'Do you think you can forgive me?' she says.

The Apologia

It was a square-looking house, blocky and plain and sharp around the edges, perched on a ratty lawn. The land sloped sharply at the back and bordered on a school field. The fence was old and made of wire, with a sunken bit in one place where the kids would cut through. There was a cabbage tree out the front, a lone gesture to decorative foliage, stooped and vaguely depressing There was the driveway, where he'd stood once, screaming for a long time. They'd locked the doors. It had gone on for a while, and then stopped. A welcome silence had oozed around the doorframe, and a bird had chirped. The children finished their crying.

That night they'd all made nachos, and her mother said to invite her friends over, as many as she wanted. The feeling inside the house then was like that inside an air-balloon basket just before take-off. The balloon was prepped and full of volatile gas, the edges of the basket inching off the ground and then jolting downwards, the balloon almost, but not quite, leaving the ground.

Most days when she came home from school there was a smell inside the house: mould overlaid with too many cleaning products. It was the cheapest place they could find. Everything was polished and ironed, perfectly hanging in time. The brown seventies carpet and beige curtains, the nets in the windows like bridal veils, the mottled vinyl surface of the kitchen bench. There was a window between the lounge and the hallway made of dark orange glass. There were murky lampshades, with tassels. Everything was achingly clean and scrubbed. The hallway was always cold but look – right now there's sunlight streaming onto the couch in the lounge room and the TV is on and it's her mother's favourite show and there, the sun is falling right onto a pile of clean, freshly folded washing. Her mother's, the baby's, the other kids'.

'We're poor,' her mother said. 'We're poor now, but at least we've always been clean.'

He sipped his coffee, took a bite of tiropita.

'And when the Turks invaded the city of Smyrna,' he said, 'when they occupied and burned and massacred the Greek Orthodox Christians and the Armenians of Smyrna, this is in 1922,' he threw his arms around, 'and it was a holocaust, one that the world still has not properly acknowledged, you understand. There were hundreds of Christians slaughtered. When they invaded, it wasn't an occupation. It was genocide.'

She's uncomfortable at the table. It's warm in the café and the air is fugged with the smell of other people's breakfast eggs. She's in her favourite clothes, brown corduroy pants, boots, an op-shop shirt. When she had told her mother she was going to see him her mother hadn't answered for a long moment. And then she'd looked her up and down, fussed at her collar, brushed at her shorn, boyish hair.

'You could at least wear something nice,' she said. 'Show him we're not beggars.'

'Mum.'

'I don't know why you insist on wearing that sort of thing. You look like a hobo.'

'Mum!'

'If you're not back within an hour, I'm calling the police.'

'You need to understand, I'm telling you this because it was covered up and they still haven't taken responsibility for this travesty and this massacre but we know,' he said, sipping his latte, 'we *know*, we *remember*, that's what you have to learn about your people. We are a people who *remember*.'

She paused, took a sip of coffee. When she brought her cup back to the saucer it rattled slightly. She looked him carefully in the eye.

'It was my understanding that the Turks did apologise,' she said.

He looked at her, his eyes moving rapidly. He was sometimes capable of being handsome, but now his colour was high, and in the heat his face was florid. She looked more like him, she knew, with her black hair and dark eyes, her soft, rounded face. Every morning when she looked in the mirror she wished for her mother's sharp cheekbones, that face certain of its own direction in the world, not this sulking moon of hers. She would shave off the edges of her face if she could, so that it matched how she felt. She would chisel her real self out of this blurred mass till she looked hard and real, directional, less like a thing that was acted upon.

'Yes, but for so long it was covered up,' he said, 'with the complicity of the Anglo-dominated Western world. And when they did apologise, it was a token apology. They only did it because of international pressures. There were no reparations offered. No proper apologia. Understand,' he said, 'I'm only telling you all this because I see your mind working away in there and God knows you're a beautiful girl, but I see you have a good mind too, a critical little mind. There's a few of us in the family – thinkers. That's how we're similar, you and I.'

Something happened in her body. She might throw up or burst. But she kept her eyes steady on him. Her mind was critical, but little. She was beautiful but could also think. What did that even mean? They were similar, she and him.

The waitress came over to check on everything.

'Everything's great, thank you, sweetheart,' he said. He stared hard at her departing form. The waitress looked back, straight at her. She was pinned to her chair. She was sure her face was red. The waitress's ponytail swished lushly. She was a couple of years older than her, just out of school. The waitress didn't raise her eyebrow. She didn't have to. She came back, filled her water glass, and put the jug on the table, in front of him, without filling his glass. He didn't notice.

'It was done with no honour. They invaded at night, they snuck in the back door. It was carefully planned. The Greeks and Armenians, they had no warning, no chance to defend themselves. It wasn't an honest fight.'

She sipped her coffee. Her mother didn't let her drink coffee. In his current mood, he would buy her whatever she wanted, as long as it conflicted with her mother's rules. She should ask for a bottle of vodka.

'Like how we left you?' she asked. 'In the middle of the night, so you didn't have a chance to stop us?'

Afterwards, she was picked up by her friends in a bright yellow Toyota Corolla filled with cigarette smoke. Her friends waved to him obnoxiously as they pulled away, in a way that could only just be construed as friendly. They knew all about her father. For a moment she felt sorry for him. A critical little mind.

She texted her mother.

'No need to call the police. I'm with Phillip, Kelly and Jen. Back tonight. Don't worry about my dinner.'

Her mother texted back.

'Was he alright?'

Not 'Are you alright?' but 'Was he alright?'

Someone was rolling her a cigarette out of a pouch of tobacco. Someone was lighting it for her. She cracked open the window, blew out a smooth stream of bitter smoke. This could mean: 'Did he behave appropriately?' but it probably meant 'Was he okay?'

There was time, amidst the worst of it, when they left her alone in the house, in the wee hours of the morning. He'd had enough, he said. He'd had it up to here with them. There was the usual scuffle, in which she attempted to intervene. He went off furiously, on foot. It was a work night.

Her mother left her with the children, and the baby, who was awake. She drove off to look for him, afraid he wouldn't come back, afraid he would get lost or do something to himself. Most of all, her mother feared her father's job being put in jeopardy – the ensuing scandal if her father didn't turn up to work, if the marriage broke up, if it all came out.

The baby was breastfed and kept crying and snuffling at her flat chest. The second youngest wouldn't go down.

'Why don't we all get into my bed?' she said loudly, over the baby's cries. 'I'll read a book, and we can have a sleepover!' They crept in, one by one, but the second youngest had wet herself in the confusion and needed changing. She gave the baby to her brother, who looked blankly at its wide-open mouth.

'Just bounce her,' she said.

'I'm tired,' her brother said. He laid the baby on the bed, where it continued to scream.

She read to them until they fell asleep. She stayed awake. If she slept, she thought, she might roll onto the baby and suffocate it, or one of them might fall out and, in crying, wake the others. She watched the blinds for any sign of headlights. Her body was as alert as if it was first thing in the morning, and she was taking an exam. It was a test. She had to keep her eyes open. She had to know when they arrived, prepare herself for the opening of the door. Her brother's foot slipped out from under the covers and she covered it quickly, as though leaving it outside the blankets would mark her as negligent. No-one could say that she hadn't kept them warm. Their collective breath made the windows mist at the edges, till the condensation ran down in drops.

It was close to morning when her mother returned. Her father was with her, mute and pale and silent.

'He's had a hard time,' her mother said to her, before they all went to bed.

'Hey!' Her friend Phillip was speaking. 'Hey, man, you were totally somewhere else. So I guess it wasn't great?'

'Seeing Dad?' She wished she had some other word for him. 'I guess not.'

There was a moment where none of her friends spoke, and the tinny pop on the radio triumphed. It was a cheap stereo, and only played AM stations. But no-one else had a car, so no-one cared.

'Hey, guys, I think it's time for the plan,' Jen said.

'The plan?' her own voice sounded pathetic, thin. She wished she was better at acting fine.

'The plan, the plan!' Kelly was cheering, and Phillip was joining in.

'There's one thing,' Jen said to her. 'You have to agree to be blindfolded.'

'What?' She drew hard on the cigarette. She wasn't sure she was up for this.

'Come on!'

'It's a surprise…'

'We've been wanting to do it for ages…'

'Alright.' She knew if she didn't agree to it, they would hassle her forever. And what better thing was there to do?

'First, we have to have a proper smoke.' Phillip was businesslike.

'Who knows a place?'

'Who has some? How much do we have?'

She settled back into the cheap vinyl seat, and turned up the radio. She texted her mother: *He's just fine. Just the same.*

Her mother wrote back: *Good to hear.* She was probably feeding the baby, or cooking dinner. It wasn't that she didn't want to pay attention. She just didn't have any more attention left to give.

He hadn't expected her to speak plainly to him. He wasn't prepared for that, she could tell. He was endlessly amazing in his ignorance, her father. He was wholly closed, self-possessed, moving through life with a kind of blunt force. He offended people without knowing it. He got laid off from most jobs, always after some personal issue with management. He liked to challenge people directly, particularly if they were a part of three overlapping groups: the moneyed, the intellectuals, or what he liked to call the conservative Anglo mainstream. He would pick fights with anyone who might be sympathetic to same-sex couples, or environmentalists, or the unemployed. But the groups he most despised were those that comprised the white elite. She supposed it was this aspect of him that her mother had found attractive, coming as she did from her working-class immigrant background, where people spoke openly, and emotions were yelled out over the spaghetti.

They were similar, she and him, he had said.

But she knew herself to be dough-like, malleable. In some ways she felt it was her body that rendered her porous, this female form that had lately begun to betray her in its corporeal unpredictability. Of course, she resisted, when she was blamed, or when the two of them fought, and then a rage came out of her that was almost entirely unconnected to who she was. Sometimes she blacked out in the midst of her parents' fights. Her rage closed in and she could see nothing, knew nothing. She would come to, finding herself pushing her body between theirs. Or onto him. But she was not strong enough to hurt anyone. At these times his eyes always remained on her mother, and her mother's on him. She couldn't disrupt the flow of whatever had started. Her mother would push her aside, out of his trajectory. She was sure he never really saw her in such moments. She was a part of her mother, little more than that. She was never solid enough to block his hand.

The waitress came back over. She wore black skinny jeans and a torn T-shirt, and possessed an unquestionable glamour. She asked if they wanted more coffee, speaking only to her and not her father, swinging her hair over her shoulder. He ordered more of everything, even though she didn't know how he could be hungry. There was a brief interval while they waited for their coffee. He looked around as if he was in a foreign country, even though he had been the one to choose this café – Greek-owned, of course. Their coffees came and she smiled at the waitress. There was a spot of white foam at the corner of her father's mouth. She was glad it was there, glad he didn't know about it.

'Sweetie, I'm not drawing parallels here,' he said. His voice was soft. 'What your mother did, taking you and the kids from me, that was one thing. She's a good woman, your mother, don't get me wrong. I'm just talking about honour, about how the Turks ambushed the Armenians and the Greeks in the night. That wasn't an honourable act. I'm just educating you as to your history. God knows, bless his holy name, no-one else is going to.'

She reached over to his plate and took a forkful of his tiropita. He watched her lift it to her mouth. It was delicious.

'They came in the night and they burned their houses. Some escaped; many didn't. But I wanted to tell you a story about the women.'

She cut another piece off his pie, lifted it to her plate. He considered not sharing food an Anglo-Saxon flaw. He wouldn't challenge her.

'In Smyrna, fire spread through the city. The Turks, God forgive them for they knew not what they did, they were looting, burning, murdering the Armenians and the Greeks in their beds. And the women of the city they got up, and they started to clean.'

They went to a reserve and smoked until their talk scattered and spread and filled the inside of the car, and time stopped working normally. The top of her head felt it might come right off at the merest provocation. She heard her own laughter, disembodied, moving up and away across the ceiling to where it fell in with the others' in a tinkling pool. The others! She loved them passionately, gratefully, oh, how she loved them.

'It's time,' Jen said.

'Time for the blindfold.'

'Blindfold her! Do it!'

If she had loved them less, trusted them less, it would have been frightening. But she accepted the scarf that Kelly strapped across her eyes. With sight gone, she had expected the other senses to be heightened, but they weren't. Instead she felt cut off from everyone, half-deaf as well, and strangely incapable of speech, as though the barrier installed was a body-sized dome rather than a blindfold. She shifted on the seat as they careened around a roundabout, her body loose and reactive without the benefit of sight. Her friends whooped and yelled. She realised they were going around again, and again, so that she soon lost any idea of what direction she was facing, of where she was.

'Alright in there?' Jen asked.

'Yes.' Her voice was oddly formal.

'Ciggie?'

Kelly handed her a smoke she must have rolled. Someone lit it. Suddenly, she was free, absolutely and luxuriously. Malleable, permeable, but unafraid. This was her, absolutely vulnerable, open to wherever they were taking her, and entirely safe.

They drove for a long time. She had no idea where she was, but she knew Phillip was driving down odd side roads, taking the most circumlocutory route he could find. It seemed to go on for hours. Finally, the car stopped, and Phillip cut the engine.

'Take off the blindfold,' he said.

When she got home that night she was late, much later than she had ever been before. It was a school night, and her mother was up waiting, her face pinched and strained.

She put her bag on the table and waited for the onslaught. She wasn't nervous about her mother smelling smoke on her. Her friends had visited this house a lot in various states of inebriation, and they had established that her mother had a talent for wilful ignorance. 'What's up with her?' Kelly had said once. 'If I came home with red eyes and raided the pantry stinking of smoke my mother would be all over it. Does she really just not know?' She had avoided answering. Her place became a favourite for hangouts and snacks, her mother always welcoming but busy with one thing or another. 'It's like she can't really see us,' Jen said. She hadn't answered this either.

But tonight her mother was angry.

'Where have you been?'

'Where I told you I was. With my friends.'

'I didn't say you could stay out so late.'

'You didn't say I couldn't.'

'You can't stay out this late on a school night. You'll ruin your studies.'

She couldn't help it; she laughed. It burst out of her, a laugh so loud it might wake the children in this thin-walled house, where they slept two or three to a room. A laugh that could turn into something else. But she didn't let it change, she kept on laughing.

Her mother's face went slack, and then, quickly, she composed it.

'You haven't even apologised!'

'Apologise!' she said. 'Apologise!' It was a hilarious word, a foreign word. What was it he had said? An apologia. The Turks needed to make reparations, they needed to issue a proper apologia. They needed to say sorry. 'What is it you expect me to apologise for?' She laughed some more.

After a while she noticed her mother's hands were shaking.

'I better get to sleep, Mum,' she said. The words she wouldn't speak hung between them. *I'm sorry.* She kissed her mother's cheek, the impenetrable cheek-bone, the high brow arching over it. She left her at the kitchen table and went to bed.

She was beginning to feel ill because of all the coffee. But she finished it anyway, drinking all the way to the bitter grounds at the bottom of her cup.

'The women of Smyrna knew they were defeated, but they were people of a proud race. When they heard the Turks coming they cleaned their houses. They dusted. They made sure the dishes were put away. You have to imagine, they could hear the fire coming, and the screams floating across the city. They could see the wood of the houses burning and smell the smoke. I've seen pictures. Before that, it was a pretty town. You know, the white houses, the blue water, all of that. The women of Smyrna they could smell other things burning, worse things than wood. But they didn't just leave. They cleaned their houses. Then they gathered their children and left.'

The waitress looked over at them and approached, but at the last moment something caused her to veer away and clear another table. It was at this point she realised her whole body was clenched, like a fist.

'I'm not sure where it comes from, this story,' he said. 'I heard it from my father when I was a boy. It must have come down from someone who survived. They say someone asked these women, that night, why they were cleaning. "We would not give them the pleasure of saying they have burned down a dirty house." That's what the women said.'

He looked at her. The moment grew uncomfortably long.

'Right,' she said.

'This tells you something about their pride. This tells you about their standards. "Let them say they have destroyed us," they said, "but let them not say we have lived like pigs." That is what the women of that city said, and then they put their brooms away, and closed their doors, and ran.'

When they took the blindfold off, the colours rushed into her head like an explosion. Sound was back, and touch, and she herself was back, real and present and sitting here in her own, perfect, flawed body, her hand holding a cigarette and braced against the car door, the light falling into her eyes at hyper speed, making her blink.

From her place in the front seat she could see a wide, almost featureless, field. Because she had been deprived of sight, the green of the grass was glowing uproariously, the few small flowers proclaiming their obscene yellowness. The sky was a slate grey, and in the distance she could see the graffitied walls of warehouses, some kind of old industrial complex.

'Are you ready?' Phillip asked.

'What's the time?' Kelly asked.

'It's time. Don't worry,' Jen said. They were nervous. She didn't understand why – surely in losing her this thoroughly, in bringing her to this surreal, open landscape, which they had somehow found so close to their ugly, built-up city suburb, they had already achieved something.

She was about to exclaim how beautiful it all was, the field, the open sky, when she heard the train.

The sound came from the left, and when she squinted, she saw the straight line cutting across the grass was a train track. It was old, and seemingly unused. Her friends were silent, watching her for a reaction. The train grew louder and louder, but she could see no train. It should be coming up the tracks but it wasn't; it simply wasn't there. It was louder and it was louder and then it was passing, but still, she could not see it. It was there, undeniably, but it was formless, invisible.

When it had passed, and the sound had completely gone away, she found that her mouth was hanging open.

They waited for her to speak. At length, Phillip broke the quiet.

'Pretty awesome, right?'

They waited.

'Guys,' she said. She found now that she was crying freely, the tears moving down her cheeks without a sound. 'It was perfect.'

Many years later, she asked Jen, with whom she was still in touch, where the field was. Jen wouldn't say.

'But what was the deal with the train?' she asked. 'The ghost train?'

Over the years she had considered many theories. The train must have passed behind the distant warehouses, only seemingly passing in front of them. Or there was another track behind the car, somehow concealed. The sound was an aberration caused by the architecture of the place, some weird conspiracy of echoes.

'We just wanted to give you a buzz. We promised,' Jen said, hand over her heart, 'that we would never tell you.'

She supposed she could have gone looking for it herself, that strange urban field hidden somewhere in the city. But she never did.

'Pride is a tricky thing,' he said. 'A good amount of it is valuable, but then there are those that have too much of it. You're a smart girl, that's why I'm telling you,' he said. 'It can backfire on you, pride, it can be dangerous.'

The waitress came and cleared their dishes. She swept a cloth across the table directly in front of him, though there were no crumbs there. They rose to leave. The girl half-smiled at her, and she ducked her head. He took care of the bill, and then went on as though he'd never stopped.

'Pride makes you angry. It makes you take risks with the things you love. But it pays to have a little pride, in this world. Or else, people, they take you for granted.'

'You might want to look at getting some help,' she said. 'You might want to do some thinking about the things you've done to us.'

She looked into his open face, his moon face, in which the anger was now rising. She could almost feel its heat.

'If you don't sort yourself out, I won't see you again,' she said. 'And when the kids get old enough to decide, they won't want to see you either.' She walked out the door ahead of him, into the street.

When he came outside, he wore a puzzled expression. He stood awkwardly by her side, half-looking into her face, half, it seemed, afraid to look. When she got into the car, she caught him squinting at her as she closed the door, studying her intently, as if he was for all the world trying to figure out where he had seen her before. As if he was trying to work out who she was.

The Free Box

The day Belle saw her father was the day we became best friends.

We'd known each other before, but after that there was something between us, some unspoken thing that was there when we were around other people, something I understood about her that they didn't. Belle was a circus performer; we'd met at the Women's Circus where I was doing lighting and she was on trapeze. Everyone loved Belle. She was cute and small and neat; she flipped and somersaulted on the bar like nothing I'd ever seen.

When I saw Belle that first night, I thought she looked like a tulip. She had big green-brown eyes and a delicate little mouth, and her skin was pale and smooth. I was in charge of training the lights on her and it was strange, I can tell you, flicking them from gold to red to gold again, changing the colour of her skin as she pranced on the trapeze. The crowd was going off, but she seemed impervious to it all, contained, lithe in her lycra and spinning like a toy.

She came to meet me afterwards.

'I'm Belle,' she said, extravagantly, generously. She shook my hand. Her spandex was hot pink, and she wore fishnets underneath. When she spoke, you felt she was giving you a present.

'Tora,' I said. I was dusty from the beams, and hot. I looked down.

'It's hard work, on the lights,' Belle said. 'I did some lighting a couple of years ago, but I gave it up. Too many men in the industry.'

'Yeah, I know!' I was surprised. 'The producers and the managers, they're mostly guys. No-one thinks I can lift anything.'

'But you're great!' Belle said. She smiled. 'That's what I came to say, the lighting was totally spot on. You timed it with the changes in the music and everything!' She sighed dramatically. 'God, you don't know how long I've waited for a lighting person like you.'

I noticed a blue sequin glued to her cheek at the corner of her eye.

The day Belle saw her father, she'd come round to my house for a cup of tea. I'd been stencilling words onto T-shirts. I was planning to sell them at the local fair. I had on painty jeans and a bandanna over my hair. Belle arrived with biscuits and as we ate them I showed her the T-shirts.

'I just love this one, Tora,' she said, holding it up. '2 Rad 4 Brands' – that's awesome.'

'Thanks,' I said, looking down at the shirt. It was just a T-shirt. I only made them to amuse myself. I didn't expect anyone to like them.

'I'd love to make more stuff,' Belle said. 'Like you. Patches and stuff.'

'Hey, did you know there's a free box outside that place down the road?' I asked. 'At that new op shop? I had a look yesterday. There's heaps of free material and stuff.'

'A free box!' Belle smiled. 'We should go check it out.'

The day outside was clear and still. It seemed earlier than it was, like the air wasn't dirtied by people's breathing yet. There was no wind. The blossoms were coming out on the trees along my street and we heard a Howler monkey call as we left the house, from the zoo one street away. Even the council flats at the end of the road looked clean and crisp, lucid in the light. It was weird that the zoo was in the city; one year a lion escaped and had to be brought back home. Gangs lived in the flats next to the platypus enclosure, and the peacock calls sounded over the city sirens.

'So how are you?' Belle asked.

I sighed. 'I'm having a hair crisis.'

Belle looked at me. 'You want to shave it off again?'

'Yeah. I don't know what it is, I just get this urge. But then whenever I do it I get hassled at work.'

Belle did a little skip. She was wearing a petticoat and turquoise cardigan; her hair was cut in a pixie style and she'd dyed it fire-engine red.

'It's just fashion,' she said. 'Humans are essentially superficial, right? Don't worry about it! Do whatever you want, Tora. I think you'd look great with a shaved head!' She flung her arms wide and did a few tap-dance steps on the street, her shoes crunching on some broken glass. She spun. She laughed.

'It's political,' I said. She rolled her eyes, still dancing, arms out to the world.

We were coming back along the main road when we saw him.

We'd passed the point where the shops petered out into old houses, past the mural of the stars and moon on the side of a building, past the second-hand book-shop and the community centre. Someone had sprayed graffiti on its wall: *It could be worse, you could be on fire.* We were stepping lightly past the TAB with the cigarette butts and beer cans on the verge outside, the Asian food store with its smell of samosas wafting out. Belle was carrying a huge pile of fabric she'd got from the free box, polka-dotted and striped and patterned material wrapped around with a scarf. I had a smaller pile. We were going to make patches and sew them onto things.

'We're so resourceful,' Belle said to me. She winked.

'I would have been good in the Depression,' I said.

We started to cross the road. There was a man coming towards us, a non-descript man muffled up in layers of clothing. He had a beanie on, pulled low over his eyes, and a huge baggy jacket, loose pants. He was staring at Belle. People tend to stare at Belle. She hadn't seen. I waited for him to call some random insult, or a pick-up line. You can get anything round here.

We were halfway across the street when he spoke.

'Hello,' he said.

He didn't speak to me but directly to her. We were pretty close to him by then, standing almost face to face.

Belle stopped walking and stood there, still, fabric trailing from her arms.

'Dad,' she said then. 'Dad.'

I watched her face empty of everything, the things she had been about to say, what kind of patches she would make, the moves she would perform tonight at the circus, everything. The smile slowly left her face.

'I didn't recognise you,' she said.

'Hi,' the man said. 'Hi, honey.' His voice was low and gentle; I could hardly hear it over the traffic sounds. 'I thought I'd see you sometime, Belle,' he said. 'I thought I'd run into you one of these days.'

Belle stepped forward suddenly and clasped him, the scraps pressed between their bodies, his big dark coat against her red hair. A car turned into the street and nosed towards us. It tooted its horn.

'Come on,' I said to them. 'Come on! We have to get off the road.'

They moved as if hypnotised. They didn't look at me.

'I meant to call you,' Belle said. 'I meant to, I had this phone number, but then it didn't work and—'

'It's okay,' the man said.

I couldn't see any resemblance between them, but then I saw his eyes were similar, a slightly darker shade of brown than hers. I realised he was crying.

When I turned to look at Belle there were tears on her face too.

'It's okay, Belle,' the man said again. 'What you been up to, honey? What you been doing?'

Belle gasped a little. 'You know, Dad,' she said. Her face wasn't scrunched up or red at all, the tears were just something happening naturally, like breathing. 'This and that. Performing. Travelling a bit. I live down there!' she said, pointing with one arm and clutching her bundle with the other. 'How about you?'

'I'm alright,' Belle's father said. 'I been working, it's a little job, really, but it's something. I'm local again, so,' he said. He reached into his pocket, scribbled a note on a piece of card. He was still crying, those Belle-eyes watery in his face. 'So here's my number,' he said. 'Honey, if you want to give me a call. When you're ready.'

He gave it to her.

'Thanks,' Belle said. 'Thanks, Dad.'

He kissed her cheek and walked across the road, away from us.

Belle looked at me as if she were waking up, and saw me there, waiting.

'Tora! Sorry,' she said. 'I'm so sorry, I just...'

'No, Belle, don't be stupid,' I said. 'It was your dad. I don't mind! God,' I said.

We started to walk. The tears kept running down Belle's face in the clear light, like jewels. I put my arm around her.

'I haven't seen him in three years,' she said. 'And you know the horrible thing? It's not even like we had some big fight or anything. I went down south and then he had to move,' she said. 'He had some debts or something, got in trouble with the police. And it's not like he talks to Mum.' She took a breath. I looked at her. She was hugging the scraps of fabric to her chest.

'I kept meaning to call him but then it got awkward, you know, because I'd left it so long.' She stopped suddenly. 'Oh God,' she said. 'I forgot to say I missed him, didn't I? I forgot to tell him!'

'It's alright,' I said. 'I'm sure he knows.' He'd spoken to her so softly, weeping in the middle of the road.

We started walking again. I could smell the blossoms on the trees near my house.

'He looked so different,' she said. 'For the longest time, standing there, I didn't recognise him.'

We'd been walking together, but now I let her go and looked at her. She was stepping without seeing the footpath, the material bunched up under her chin, looking up at the sky.

'Let me carry that for you,' I said. I reached over and gathered up the fabric. She let it go, not looking, the material cascading into my hands.

She rubbed her face with the back of her hand. She swung her arms.

I hefted the load up, trying not to drop it. All the bright colours, the musty smell.

'Thanks,' she said. 'I didn't realise.' She smiled at me. 'I didn't realise how heavy it was.'

The Presence Chamber

It wasn't what happened at the birth. It was the needing to continue, afterwards.

The eyes of the women at kindergarten followed Sarah with infinite sympathy. They had never dreamed of something like this, they wanted to express. They had always dreamed of it. They couldn't imagine. They had all imagined. It was all too visceral for them, as if she was a weal of fresh blood trailing into the room, dripping down someone's leg. As if she was the wound left after an accident, profane and unforgivable, a scar.

The kinder was everything they'd wanted – organic, with chooks, inclusive, with a community feel, in the middle of Brunswick. It wasn't a baby factory. That was what they all told each other, as they chatted after drop-off, expressing great interest in the working bees and the fundraising dinners.

It took some time to physically recover. Sarah's parents came, and her parents-in-law. They all took turns entertaining her first child, who was spinning out there in a void somewhere on his own, on the edge of understanding. Jacob was four years old, and for months she had been talking to him about his baby sister to come. He would greet her after kindergarten by embracing her stomach. He would kiss the bump in front of the other mothers. The women would look at her, their eyes filled with a bovine happiness.

'It's the best thing in the world, isn't it?' one woman said. 'It's the best thing you'll ever do.'

Another woman at the kindergarten had put a hand on her arm.

'It's good you're having another,' she said. 'Only children are the worst.' She had two older girls at the private school down the road, and she said only children couldn't help being selfish. She said that Jacob would have ended up self-centred, unless he was forced to share. It was good that Sarah was having a second child, and just in time, too. You didn't want too big a gap.

Sarah was close to some of the mothers. Blond Marion, with the twin toddlers and an older child. Sheree, with the thick black bangs and red lipstick and laughing eyes. They spoke intensely to each other, in the harried space of the kindergarten playground. They spoke urgently, like young girls exchanging information about something important: leg-shaving or body odour. In this way Sarah learned that Marion'd had a caesarean at thirty-two weeks with the twins, that Sheree'd had three 'normal' births, and that Judy was an avid homebirther and anti-vaxxer. They discussed epidurals and active labour and risk factors. They discussed the point in their labours when they'd all felt out of control, like it could not humanly be done.

'It's counterintuitive, isn't it?' Marion said. 'You have to move towards the pain.'

'It's brutal,' said Sheree. 'Nothing can prepare you for it.'

Judy the homebirther had taken no pain relief during her labours, Marion said. She looked at them carefully, sidelong.

Sarah, who'd had a 'typical' birth with Jacob, in which she had chosen an epidural ten hours in, nodded. Sheree rolled her eyes.

'The demands we put on ourselves,' she said. 'I didn't have pain relief with my three, but only because the doctors weren't quick enough. I was screaming for the needle.'

Sarah and Brian had tried for two years for this baby, but where Jacob's conception had been easy, this second one had evaded them. They were both checked out and declared healthy; it just happened like that sometimes, the doctors said. Sarah had mastered the statistics on conception, and all the while Jacob grew. Next year he would be starting school.

'Judy calls contractions *rushes*,' Marion said.

Sarah, who felt this might be going too far, looked at Judy, where she was chatting with the kindergarten supervisor. She didn't wear Birkenstocks or dreadlock her hair. Before having her children, she had worked in a bank.

'I called them rushes too,' Sarah said. 'When I was preparing for Jacob's birth. I'd read a book that said if you used positive language it would make a difference.'

Now all of the women rolled their eyes.

Sheree's youngest boy approached and pointed at Sarah's belly.

'Do you have a baby in there?' he asked. 'Are you going to push it out?'

'She's going to push it out of her vagina,' said Jacob, proudly. He had come up behind them. The women laughed.

'I've tried to teach him the correct terminology,' Sarah said.

Jacob put his hand on her stomach and looked up at her with his bright, wide eyes.

'Is Baby kicking?' he asked. The baby, who Sarah felt knew his voice, kicked. Jacob ran off to play on the slide.

Marion put her head to one side and smiled.

'I'm so excited for you,' said Sheree. She put her hand on Sarah's stomach, where the baby was rolling. She sighed. 'I'd have another if I didn't realise that was batshit crazy.' She moved off with her double pram, seeking the youngest: he had fallen into the water-play pit and needed to be rescued.

Afterwards, when people touched her, it was as if they were reaching across a vast distance. Even Brian and Jacob.

People said all the usual things. People said I'm so sorry and I can't imagine. People said things happen in life, and to the best people too sometimes, and that didn't make any difference. People said, after a while, that she was doing well. She's coping, she heard them say, the voices creeping into the space that opened around her at the playground, at the kindergarten. She's coping, poor thing.

Jacob was angry. He began to hit Sarah and Brian. He often forgot what had happened and would ask when the baby was coming. Then he would ask where the baby had gone. Brian and Sarah had decided they would not hit Jacob, even though they themselves had been disciplined that way. When Jacob hit Brian, his father held him at arm's length, but Sarah saw the anger moving and shifting in his face.

'Why would he listen to me if he knows there's no real consequence?' he said to Sarah. 'My dad would have belted me, but at least I respected him.'

Brian had cried at the cremation, but not since then, to her knowledge.

A lot of people said other things to Sarah in the days after the birth. They weren't talking to her so much as to the people around her, who, it seemed, must now take care. It was as if she was something delicate that needed padding and swaddling, not this mess of stiches and raw nerves that they had poked with needles, interrogated physically, tugged on, cut into, drugged, stabbed. As if she was instead the baby, which had been taken away.

Afterwards, she read the papers. Other people had it worse, she thought. If she was a woman living in Victorian times, for example, she might have had six of her children die. Or if she lived elsewhere now even, in another country.

After a time, her parents went home. The parents-in-law went home. Brian went back to work. It was just her and Jacob. He had ceased being angry and begun to be normal again, though at times he would scream and scream, his face scrunching into that of a much younger child. At these times she didn't know what to do. He didn't want to be held.

People told her not to blame herself, but she knew that by the end of the day, when she was tired and wanted to lie down, when she was thinking about Isla, only about Isla, and the too-small urn they had been given, and the too-small pile of ashes that had floated away on the waves at the beach that Isla had never seen and never would see, that Jacob knew she was preoccupied. How could he not sense it?

When she came back to the kinder no-one asked what had happened. Women looked at her and spoke and their eyes filled with tears. Some cried helplessly while she remained dry-eyed.

Risk management, the doctors said. Post-traumatic counselling. Mindfulness, movement, yoga, exercise, support group, therapy.

One day she found a mention in the paper of an echo chamber. She was unfamiliar with the term. She asked Brian about it. He looked up, surprised.

'Oh, it's just some media thing,' he said. 'When you get caught in a feedback loop of your own making. Like on social media. All the news you see is chosen by you, so it reinforces what you already think. It can happen in real life too. You're caught in a group of people with similar beliefs. You end up thinking everyone has the same values.'

'Oh,' she said. Somehow, she'd thought it was something different, a term describing a sense of being trapped in time, of repeating the same loops over and over. Somehow, she was disappointed.

Everyone talks about time. Time heals. Time will make it easier. Give yourself time. You just need some time.

'Do you have people to talk to?' the doctors asked. She talked to Sheree, she talked to Marion. She told them the things she could not say to Brian.

She said, 'It's just crazy that she doesn't exist anymore.'

She said, 'Sometimes I think she's out there in the water, and no-one's keeping her warm.'

She said, 'Where did she go?'

Their eyes reached out to her, but some self-preserving thing inside them pulled away.

One day, at the kindergarten, Judy gave Sarah a business card.

'I heard what happened, she said. I heard what the doctors did to you. If you want a homebirth for the next one, this is the number of a good midwife. She's totally anti-intervention.'

As soon as Judy had walked away Sarah threw the card into the bin. She could not tell Judy what the doctors had said. Sarah might not be able to have any more children.

Time was a chamber that fluctuated in size. It could double or triple, when, for example, you were lying sleepless in the night thinking of the curve of your baby's ear, unlike any other baby's ear in the world. Or it could halve itself, when you were meant to be picking up Jacob but instead found yourself at the shore again, the ashes in your hands, wanting to take them into your body, wanting to consume them.

One day the papers said that scientists had discovered the actual cells of children inside their mothers' brains, years after the mothers had carried them.

'Don't you understand what this means?' Sarah said to Brian. 'This means I have her in me. This means I'm still carrying a part of her around!'

Brian looked at her uneasily. But when she told Marion and Sheree, they understood.

'You'll always have her,' Sheree said. 'She hasn't gone anywhere. She's with you.'

But she wasn't.

Judy the homebirther was pregnant again. She had no morning sickness and was glowing. She told everyone she was going for her third homebirth. It was all about your attitude, she said. It was about being in tune with your body. It was all about being in the right headspace and being confident. It was a natural process. Women had been doing it for thousands of years. She said this within Sarah's hearing, as they stood admiring the new play area.

Marion looked at Judy with disgust. Sheree took a step forward, until she was right in front of Judy, centimetres from Judy's growing belly.

'Judy,' Sheree said, 'just shut the fuck up.' Her bangs bounced fervently, and her lipsticked mouth clenched around the words. Judy's expression opened up, as if she was looking at something distasteful, but interesting. She stepped backwards, trampling the organic strawberries.

'Judy,' Sheree said, 'sometimes I just want to punch you in the face.'

That night, as Sarah told Brian, she laughed and laughed.

When Jacob was being tucked in, she heard him asking his father: 'Is Mummy okay now?'

'I'm not sure,' Brian said. 'Maybe.'

'Is she more okay than she was before?'

Sarah heard Brian go quiet. Finally, she heard a plaintive sound. Brian was crying.

Nothing changed, of course. The space was still there around her. She knew she carried Isla inside her, alive, some weird chimera inside her brain. And everywhere, as always, the sound of the sea unravelled her, over and over again.

The Conservation of the Stars

The thing rose from the structure. At first he could not make out anything but a blank form, the outline of its head and eyes against the sky. It was reptilian, simian, oddly royal. His boots were melted into the sand, his feet sweating but forgotten, his body immobilised. The head turned and he got the child behind him. He would be proud of this, later. It wasn't something he would speak of; he wasn't that kind of person. But you never knew how you would react in a crisis. You never knew what your body would do, whether it would freeze or make itself useful, whether it would be courageous or try to run.

He didn't know it then, but he would return to this moment again and again in dreams, the hot sun, Illuwantji's quick glance at him as they saw it, direct, frank, amazed, and for once, unreserved. It was a lizard, a dragon, a dinosaur. It moved and shifted and perceived them, pinning them with eyes he could now see were a pale, alien green. It had a razor-sharp hook for a beak. As it moved, he clutched the boy firmly behind him with both hands. They were directly underneath it.

It studied them, casually. It must have heard them coming but had made no move to leave. Its wings began to unfurl, jet black against the light and massive, its wingspan metres wide. He wasn't sure if he gasped or not. He thought afterwards that Illuwantji would have been silent, and the boy too. Its opening wings shifted the world around it so that his concept of space and size changed. Its shape burned into his retina, the colours of the land going lurid and hyperreal.

It was as if the air contracted. Red, ochre, orange, bright translucent blue, the colours too vivid and saturated, all somehow pulled into this too-symmetrical shape.

It rose in the nest and stood, wings fully extended, adjusting itself slightly in the breeze, looking down at them coolly, as if in consideration.

He stepped back. As though he had tripped a switch, the thing began moving, gracefully, but with an unquestionable power, towards them.

The desert was as different from Rua's home as Mars was different from the Earth. There was the dryness, the broadness of the large expanse, its inconceivable distance from the land's edge.

'Welcome to paradise.'

The man who picked him up at the airport was weathered and creased. He wore a hat with an actual flynet, something Rua assumed was decorative until they walked out of the air-conditioned airport and into the fly-ridden heat. The man was with a teenage boy whom he introduced as Kumana. Rua tried to shake his hand but the boy did not look at him or speak.

'I'm Simon,' the man said as he loaded Rua's bags into the four-wheel drive. 'Don't mind him, he's just being respectful. You tired?'

Rua had travelled for twenty hours, on three different flights, to get here from New Zealand.

'Nah,' he said. 'I'm alright.' He was high on adrenaline and coffee and the land itself. So, he thought, the colours weren't photoshopped after all. The heat was heavy and his clothes stuck to his body. He moved as if through smoke. Looking at Simon's desert boots and khaki shorts, his loose white shirt, he felt inappropriately dressed, his city shoes awkward on the gravel.

'Can you drive a troopy?'

Rua realised the man was talking about their vehicle. He shook his head.

Simon sighed despairingly, but not without humour. 'I see we have our work cut out for us.'

Rua grinned. 'You mean you fellas actually work out here? Thought I'd signed up for a year-long holiday.'

He got a smile, rather than a laugh, but it was something.

They stopped for water and supplies. Rua tried to memorise everything for when he would do the airport run in the future. Check the water, air pressure, tyres. Twenty litres of water for each person. GPS and sat-phone check, in case the car broke down. Spare food and provisions. Tools. Check the first aid kit. While Simon loaded the car, Kumana looked at him and then cast his eyes quickly down again.

'Simon's a good driver,' he said, as if answering a question Rua had asked. His voice was so soft Rua had to lean back to hear him. 'He'll get us there quickways. No worries.'

The journey took five hours down an unsealed track. Simon drove off the sides of the track to avoid the ruts. A dingo flashed in front of them. The land passed, and passed, without a house or a shop or a person or a building, as far as they could see. The scenery was uniform: desert grass, the red track ahead, the low-lying brush. The light began to fail. Simon drove faster, the dust buffeting the windows and the speedometer needle creeping up. He seemed to be looking for something.

Rua heard a sound from the back seat, a brief aspiration. Kumana's eyes were fixed on a spot on the horizon, the whites glowing. He stared at the point, his head following it as if magnetised.

'That's it,' Simon said, glancing at Kumana and then back at the track. 'The top of the radio tower.'

Rua squinted. Far away was a tiny point of light, the only one visible in the widening dark, like a lighthouse.

'That's Kumana's homelands, up ahead,' Simon went on. 'Bet you're glad to see those after a week in Melbourne, aren't ya, son?'

Kumana made no comment.

'Kumana's been spinning tunes at a city festival. I went with him.' He made a sound in the back of his throat like he was going to spit. 'All that traffic! Wouldn't live in a place like that if you paid me a million a year. The tower's attached to the media centre,' Simon said. 'Welcome home.'

Rua couldn't decide if the man meant to sound sarcastic or not.

The thing rose. It was reptilian, simian, oddly royal. He got the child behind him. It was a lizard, a dragon, a dinosaur. Its shape burned, the colours of the land going lurid and hyperreal beyond it.

Nanarkjitju was a town of about a hundred people. He had expected it to be built on ancestral lands, like the settlement around his own marae, but the people were settled in prefabricated houses in an old mining village. When he asked about the mines, the people looked away. When he tried to visit his neighbours' houses, the people seemed embarrassed for him. When he spoke to the older women though, they were friendly, like his aunties. They would hassle and joke. But the younger women passed him as though he didn't exist.

'Missionaries, misfits and miscreants,' the office lady told him on his first morning. 'Those are the three kinds of people you'll find out here. Are you Christian?'

'Not particularly.'

'Then you must be a misfit,' she said. 'Or a miscreant. I'll let you know when I figure out which one you are.' She slid a ragged folder across the table. 'Your induction info. Happy reading.'

Inside was an anthropological report on this part of the Western Desert. It was dated 1975.

Illuwantji was the first person to greet him when he arrived at the donga beside the centre. Inside were a couple of rough rooms attached to a shipping-container kitchen, the whole made of corrugated iron and cheap boards. There were bars on all the windows and wire mesh, so rocks wouldn't smash the plexiglass. Illuwantji came over, a toddler bundled under her arm. She had long, curly hair, pink at the ends where it was dyed, and a boyish frame. Her eyes were surprisingly light in her smooth-skinned face. The toddler's arm shot out to stroke his arm, the tribal tattoo he had there.

'We're in the red house,' Illuwantji said. 'You on your own in there?' she jerked her head at his donga.

'Just me,' he said. 'We might get another radio producer mid-year.'

Rua had worked his way through student radio and up, to Māori Radio. His old people had told him that he was to be an orator. But he liked to be the one holding the microphone, he'd told Simon in the Skype interview.

Illuwantji nodded.

'You might want to get yourself a dog.'

He told her he'd think about it.

Illuwantji worked at the office, often bringing a niece or nephew with her. She wore loose clothing, hoodies and jeans, but she would paint her nails. She wore plain T-shirts but plaited her hair intricately. She was a lighter colour than the locals. The office lady said she was a half-caste, that her dad was a white, and that she had grown up in the city.

'"Half-caste" would be an insult in my country.'

'You're not in your country now,' said the office lady. She winked, and offered him a biscuit.

One night the kids threw rocks at his house. He lay listening to the scattered hail, wondering whether to venture outside. Then he heard Illuwantji's voice cutting the air, hurling words he didn't understand. The rocks ceased flying.

The next day he thanked her.

'It's not their fault,' she said. 'They got nothing else to do.'

'Want to go for a walk?' he asked.

Most of the time, in Nanarkjitju, it seemed like nothing happened. But that was just a lie the heat told, the shimmering, blinding heat.

Always, he goes back to it. It was prehistoric, not something he would speak of. You never knew what your body would do. The hot, murderous sun, Illuwantji's quick glance at him as they saw it. He clutched the boy firmly behind him with both hands. The colours of the land went lurid and hyperreal.

'I don't know what I'm doing wrong,' he told Simon, after half a year.

'You're too eager,' Simon said. 'Just slow down. Give it a while longer. When they've got used to you, they'll start sharing their stories. You're just another whitey to them.'

'But I'm not white.'

Simon looked at him sharply. 'You're not local. Anyone who's not local is white. Wouldn't make a difference if you were bloody Nelson Mandela.'

'I came here to give the people a voice.'

'Honourable of you,' Simon said. He spoke quietly, almost kindly.

Rua left without answering.

The office lady shifted her glasses on her nose as he passed. She had been listening.

'Got you figured out, finally!' she said. 'You're the missionary type, after all. Here to save them. Even if you're not Christian, even if you're not white.'

Simon sent him to Yulara for supplies. He told him he had to bring someone, for safety, and that the only other person in town allowed to drive the troopy was Illuwantji.

'Don't say I never did anything for ya,' Simon said, as Rua prepared the gear. He waggled his eyebrows up and down. 'Have a drink or two for me.'

Rua couldn't help smiling.

Six hours later they were on a hill overlooking the rock. The sun had gone down, and Rua was drinking a beer. There were a few tourists, but they were hidden by a tussock. Illuwantji had said she didn't drink, not anymore.

'I come from a place on the coast,' she said. 'Tangimoana. It's a small place. You can catch crayfish there with your bare hands, collect paua. They taught me everything, about the tides, how to fish, how to dive. Tangimoana means "the sea is crying".'

Although it was late, the heat glued the backs of his knees to his jeans and he batted flies away from his face. Illuwantji did not seem bothered by them. The dry tussock stretched before them, and the stars swung above. 'You can always hear the sea, from anywhere in Tangimoana,' he said. 'You can never not hear it.'

'Some people in Nanarkjitju haven't seen the sea,' Illuwantji said. 'Some people will never see it.'

'Why'd you come back from the city?'

She paused for a long time.

'Didn't know that part of myself,' she said. 'By the time I came back, it was almost too late.'

He looked at her in surprise. 'For what?'

'My mother spoke it to me. Came back because if I have some kids, I gotta bring them up right. They gotta know where they're from, from the start.' She looked up at the sky. There they were, Minyma Kutjara, the Seven Sisters, wheeling in their quest across the sky. Even Rua recognised them now.

'You'd be a good mum.'

She gave him a special look, and smiled. She didn't often smile.

They went to bed early, in their separate rooms.

The day she suggested they go bush he agreed immediately. They drove straight out of town for a couple of hours, he, Illuwantji and a little boy of four or five. The boy was Illuwantji's 'little son', which he understood in this case meant her nephew. She was looking after him for the day. The boy went on ahead of them, but Illuwantji told him to walk in her footsteps. It was snake time, and the sun could kill you if you got lost. They walked carefully, avoiding the long grass in favour of the sand. Rua strolled, humming, his shoulders held back. Illuwantji followed behind him, smoking her rollies.

'Better wear your sunhat, whitey,' she said, though they were almost the same colour.

'What is it, do you think?' he pointed ahead at the dark mass visible on the rise. She shrugged. It was black against the sky.

'Simon said you're leaving when your contract is up,' she said.

The silence stretched out.

'Isn't that what all the whiteys do?' he said. 'Leave after a year?'

'Dunno.' He heard her sigh out the smoke, a long, calm exhale. 'Thought maybe you were different.'

Rua had thought he was too.

The structure in the tree was at least two metres across, wide and densely woven. It was a blot, a dark puzzle in the landscape. Illuwantji said she had never seen anything like it before. The weaving was sophisticated, complex. Up close, he grew confused, and when Illuwantji began to approach it a slick nervousness started up from his stomach.

'Are you sure it's okay?'

'What do you think's going to happen? Scared of the spirits?' She liked to tease him, to hold her knowledge over him. He usually didn't mind.

'It might not be a good idea, with the boy.'

'What's going to hurt him, in his own lands?' She turned away, towards the thing that blocked part of the sun. And it rose.

His feet were melted into the sand. The small boy's shoulders were clasped in his hands, his own breathing loud in the silence. Its wings, opening, shifted the world. Its shape burned into his retina, the colours of the land lurid and hyperreal. The air contracted. Red, ochre, orange, bright translucent blue.

It rose in the nest, until it stood, wings fully extended, in consideration.

He stepped back. The thing began moving gracefully towards them. Then, it leapt into the air, a heaving visual scream of feather and bone, and dived.

Rua hit the sand, the boy beneath him. Illuwantji ducked away. Then she was laughing wildly, as it soared up, wheeling once, twice, close above them, and then away.

'This is its land, see?' she said. 'It's not scared of anything!'

Rua was shaking. He got up, dusted off his shorts.

'It could have killed him.'

The boy ignored him, looking up at Illuwantji. Rua understood he wasn't the expert here.

'Walawuru. That's its name. A star eagle!' Her voice was awed. 'A guardian!' Illuwantji picked up the boy and spun him. She turned to Rua. 'It's true, it can pick up goats, hunt kangaroo. Would only take a kid though if the child was far from its people, and weak.' She looked at him closely. 'You're freaking out. Here.' It was the water bottle.

She took them higher, built a fire, boiled tea. The little boy went off to play in the sand, calm and unconcerned. In the distance they could see the bird ascending over its domain. He was shaking, but he hoped she wouldn't notice. If there would ever be a time, it would be now. She looked at him and her eyes shone out so brightly he could hardly look. He was so close to her. He could reach out and touch her arm. She would look at him, really see him. He moved, just slightly, one hand reaching for hers, but, at that moment, she shaded her eyes, following the bird's flight.

'We'll have to come back and film it,' Rua said. 'Tape your stories about it. What do your people think it means?'

Illuwantji turned to him. Her eyes went cold.

'Always wanting to put it all down,' she said. 'Like if it's not recorded it's not real. That's a sacred eagle,' she said. 'Have to ask the old people if it's okay to film it. Might not even be alright to tell people where it is.' She shook her head. 'When you going to learn you're only a ghost here?' she asked. 'You got your stories, we got ours. You can fish for our stories all you like. But they ain't got nothing to do with yours. Not in the end.'

When they came down off the hill it was getting dark. They passed the eagle rustling, back in its nest, and he felt his heart beat harder. It took all his willpower not to think of the great, black space its wings had made in the sky, divinely balanced, oddly disturbing against the wide land.

He swore to himself he would come back here, without her. He would get permission from someone. He knew the bird was important. He knew there were stories about it that were meaningful to the people, stories that were being lost. He would film it, photograph it, record its cries, capture the fine arc of its flight.

The Paper Bag

The elephant was a sickly hue when he came to stay. His skin pooled at his ankles – 'cankles', Justin called them, unsympathetically I thought – and his torso sagged in many places. He was meant to sag, of course. To sag, and roam, and meander, and bury his dead, and remember. Which is why, perhaps, he had this great surfeit of skin, as if every pore contained a memory and every line a thought about a species lost, a hunter encountered, a waterhole dried up, the memories pulling at him, till at last he would lie down, a bag of memory draped over not much else, a carcass of story.

'Cankles seems too strong a word,' I said to Justin. 'Look, there's a little definition there.' But he refused to see it.

It was an inopportune moment for the elephant to arrive, as we had two young children, and my mother-in-law was coming to stay. I didn't know where to put him in the house (it was a him, this at least was obvious), so I took to Facebook. I was part of an online group of feminist mothers that shared encouragement. We also shared our outrage. Because I no longer throw Molotov cocktails at the police, and because I have ceased to think that yelling at fascists helps to effect change, my anger has no other outlet. I, like the other white, over-educated-but-in-debt women in this group, funnelled my rage into small complaints. Molotovs are more satisfying, the sound of the impact, that gorgeous, ephemeral flame.

When I logged in, Patricia M had written that her husband wouldn't get up with the baby in the night, and that he expected her to cook for a gathering they were having that day, by default. Punk n' Nasty had said that despite agreeing to do half the household work and working the same number of hours as she did, her male partner wouldn't do the dishes. And Katriona Delight had said that her boyfriend had punched her in the face, taken the car and withdrawn all the money from their shared bank account, and that she was afraid for her life.

I sent Patricia M and Punk n' Nasty commiseration emoji. The answers to Katriona Delight's post ranged from 'Sorry you're going through this. I hope you can find the strength to heal,' to offers of money, practical help and refuge. I wrote that although I was in another city, I truly sympathised, that such behaviour was abusive, and that I hoped she could get the help she needed. The person commenting after me offered to put the boyfriend, when he appeared, in the path of a large truck.

'My MIL is arriving in a few days,' I wrote, 'and an elephant has appeared in the laundry. It's surprising. He's not really grey. He's more of an ash-lavender. We have no shared language, so I'm not sure what his requirements are. The spare room is made up for the MIL and I'm pretty sure Hubby hasn't thought about feeding the elephant, so it's all up to me. Pls halp!' This last, I hoped, would come across as light-hearted, when in fact I had spent the afternoon sobbing into the kitchen sink. But after Katriona Delight's post, my problem seemed almost insignificant. What was an elephant in the laundry to a punch in the face?

The second day, I went into the laundry to fetch some nappies, and the problem didn't seem insignificant at all. He was there, crammed into the space between the toilet stall and the washing machine. He was looking at me. His trunk swayed delicately.

'What do you want?' I asked. His big eyes blinked. 'Why are you here?' He made to back away but bumped the wall. 'Where are you going to sleep? We only have one good set of spare sheets.'

At this, his tail swept a pile of laundry off the top of the washing machine and onto the floor. Justin had put it there. 'It was too much to expect that he'd put the washing *in* the machine,' I would write later, to the mother's group. 'And turn the fucking thing *on*.' Instead, here were the crumpled socks, the dirtied underwear, scattered at the elephant's feet. His toenails needed a trim. I swept the washing off the floor and ran a load.

'I hope you're happy with yourself,' I said to the elephant. I spoke in my mother's voice, one that I now heard frequently emerging from my own mouth. 'As if I didn't have enough to do.' I slammed the door loudly behind me.

I felt fantastic, for a moment. Then I wondered if I was an animal abuser. The elephant didn't know the pressure I was under. It didn't know that my mother-in-law would consider its presence an imposition, as the elephant would divert attention away from herself. It didn't know that Justin, despite identifying himself as a feminist, considered all the dirty underwear in the house my responsibility. It was helplessly, wordlessly, an animal, and probably in distress.

I went back into the laundry, patted the elephant, and left him swaying slightly in the small room. His skin was dry and leathery, perhaps too dry, and he smelled like something alien – desert or savannah. I'd have to put moisturiser on the shopping list. But Justin had forgotten where his keys were, and the search absorbed everything for the next ten minutes, and when it was over (they were on the hook by the door), the moisturiser had escaped my mind.

When I logged into Facebook, Katriona Delight had vanished from the group, leading to a long flurry of pleas for the moderators' intervention. Down_to_F_the_Patriarchy expressed concern that the violent partner might have returned. Amelia Bedilia said she knew Katriona in person and not to worry, that she'd taken her children and left and would not be going back. Someone offered to track Katriona's partner down and give him what he deserved. A moderator posted a note about appropriate conduct online and the risks of living in a surveillance state. Amelia Bedilia said that Katriona and her children had been transported out of the city last night by women from the group. Katriona Delight's initial post would be deleted to protect her. If anyone had personal messages for her, they were to DM Amelia herself.

'The elephant is still in the laundry!' I wrote. I needed urgent advice. 'Does anyone know how I can ask him to leave, but subtly, to avoid offending it? The last thing I would want to do is make him feel unwelcome. Counting down to the MIL's stay!' Then I tried to remember what I had been doing.

'You'd forget your head if it wasn't screwed on,' my mother used to say to me. 'You couldn't organise your way out of a paper bag.' I think about this as I finick my way through the house, sorting detritus. Hairclips, staples, odd socks, screwdrivers in unsafe places. I try to be methodical. Underwear – *washing machine. Screwdriver – shed.*

But halfway through returning the objects to their homes, I found myself stalled, clutching at a doorway, with *Plastic block – toybox* and *Eggcup – kitchen cupboard* and *School notice – noticeboard + remember to make sure the money for the fundraiser is sent in an envelope with my child's name and the teacher's name on it and with the permission slip inside + write the date of the fundraiser on the calendar along with a note to make sure my child has a sunhat, extra snacks + a large water bottle + add new water bottle to the shopping list but we'll have to go to the organic co-op as there are no non-plastic water bottles at the supermarket + plastic is the enemy of the environment + all I have to pass on to my children is an inheritance of mass extinction + imminent climate change in my hands,* along with perhaps a stuffed toy and Justin's mobile phone, which he had forgotten to take to work again.

When we met, Justin was raising awareness about climate change. I was organising Reclaim the Night marches, working towards a world in which violence against women would end. Neither of these things seemed to be working out well.

Head if it wasn't screwed on. Out of a paper bag.

And my mother, on a bad day: 'One day I hope you grow up and have children who are as ungrateful as you.' Those are some of the things that have been said to me.

Here are some things that have been said about elephants: They are said to bring prowess in war. They symbolise unwieldy burdens. They are meant to mean patience and calm. Ganesha is an elephant. He is known as the great remover of obstacles.

The third day, I went into the laundry and looked the elephant in the eye.

'What is it you want me to remember?' I asked.

The elephant raised his trunk as though he might strike me.

At last! A small part of me enthused. Punch me in the face!

During our worst arguments, Justin's and mine, I would say, 'Anything would be better than your constant "forgetting".' I meant: *Do something. Give me an excuse to leave.*

He would look at me, impassive.

Justin worked full-time and had a long commute. The youngest was one and when I thought of him going to day care I started to hyperventilate. Justin would leave before it was light and arrive home in the dark. We told ourselves we were privileged.

The elephant's trunk was raised above my head. He would strike me. I would take to Facebook, and everyone would see my bruise. People would offer help. Women would come, and take me away from all of this.

The elephant's trunk hovered. A smell of savannah, and tigers, and unfamiliar leaves. It stroked my face.

I went into the lounge, chastened.

On the fourth day, Justin called me in to the laundry. The elephant had shat in the corner. Compared to the shit of the children, the elephant's shit was immense.

'What do we do?' I asked Justin. 'We can't go on like this.'

'I was meant to leave for work ten minutes ago,' Justin said.

From the other room I heard the baby start to cry. We looked at the shit.

'I think you'll have to use the garden shovel,' Justin said.

The kids had shown no interest in the elephant. I'd taken them in several times to see him, but they'd acted as if he wasn't there.

'What are you feeding him?' Melania B wrote on Facebook. 'I'm a veterinarian and, depending on the species, the elephant might not do well with GE food. You'll have to buy organic.'

After googling, I had decided that my elephant was an African elephant. Where was I going to find organic elephant food? I supposed that would be better than the grass I had been feeding him.

'That elephant should be returned to the wild,' Christini Ara wrote. 'The laundry isn't an appropriate enclosure.'

'I agree with Christini Ara!!' Lucy Tree wrote. 'But there is no appropriate enclosure for an elephant! Free the elephant!'

I slammed my laptop shut. Did anyone in the group know my actual address? They might stage an intervention. I wouldn't log in anymore.

That night, a bellow came from the laundry. When Justin and I entered the room, it was clear what had happened. The elephant had opened the washing machine and was trying to extract the wet washing that Justin had forgotten to put out that morning. The washing had a doggy stink and would need to be washed again. The washing machine lid had fallen on the elephant's trunk, trapping it.

We freed the creature. I looked into his large, human-like eye. I was sure he was trying to help. Over the last few days, the elephant had become almost translucent, his skin more lavender, glowing from within. It occurred to me that he might not be real.

'He's changed since he turned up,' Justin said. 'His features are finer, somehow.' He patted the elephant softly, the *pat pat pat* like rain on the roof.

On the fifth day, I went back online. There were comments imploring me to free the elephant, and ones attacking my character.

'I never meant to cause any harm,' I wrote. 'I acknowledge that I have limited knowledge of elephants and of their needs. I'll be calling in professionals shortly. I never meant to imply that it was okay for an elephant to be caged. Thanks for all of your input. I'm going to go and check my human privilege and my own assumptions.'

I went in to the laundry, where the elephant stood. He turned his head. I stroked his ears. They were papery and silky at the same time. He had long, lustrous eyelashes.

'Is there anything you want me to know?' I whispered into his ear. He stirred, but said nothing.

Back on Facebook, Katriona Delight's partner had found her. She needed to be moved. Amelia Bedilia wrote that Katriona needed a new place to stay until a safehouse could be located.

I DM'd her immediately.

On the sixth day, Katriona Delight and I sat in the kitchen. All the minutiae of my family's lives sat on the kitchen table and I didn't tidy it away. Instead, I offered her arnica cream for her black eye, and we drank whisky, straight. Her kids were somewhere else for the moment. She looked around in a hollow way. She had long black hair and tattoos. Her eye was a flower of purple unfolding into yellow.

She looked at the messy washing, the dirty floors. She looked at the men's underwear lying beside the kitchen table. She went to the toilet in the laundry and came back, shaking her head.

'Did you know you have an African elephant in there?' she asked.

'I don't know what to do about him,' I said. 'He won't even tell me why he's here.'

'He's been sent by the revolutionaries,' she said. 'He wants you to go with him. We've been planning this for months. You have to get out of here. Don't you remember?'

I didn't answer her. I had forgotten the moisturiser for the elephant's skin, and the fundraiser money, which was due today. I couldn't organise my way out of a paper bag.

'It's not meant to be like this,' Katriona said. 'No-one's meant to do this alone. It's not natural. You're meant to have a tribe.'

'I'm not alone,' I said. 'I have Justin. He's meant to do some housework. It's just that he works so much. Men, am I right?'

I waited for her to say he was a bastard and that I should leave him. I waited for her to say, 'Fuck the patriarchy,' and tell me that all men were useless.

She shrugged.

The last day, I woke early and went to clean out the laundry. The elephant shifted restlessly on his hind legs. He had grown more vibrant now, as if he had sucked something from within the house. His skin was light, almost luminous. I finished shovelling his shit into a bucket.His smell was different today, like the petrichor of light rain. I had thought he had come to us to die but he seemed more alive than ever.

Katriona called from the backyard. She had readied our bicycles. Our children would ride in the bike trailer. We would pick her kids up on the way. She called out that she couldn't fit my yoga mat in, and that I wouldn't need it where we were going. Once we were there, we wouldn't need our laptops either.

Justin burst through the laundry door.

He had left for work already, but now he was back. There had to be some casualties of the revolution, and I'd figured my relationship would be the first. I'd already cried into the sink.

'I can't believe you'd leave without me,' he said. His eyes were full of tears. 'I can't believe you'd think I didn't understand.' The elephant let out a great huff, and the dirty washing slumped out of its basket and onto the floor. 'I'm sorry about the fucking housework, okay?' Justin said. 'I never wanted to work like this. But when the kids were born—'

'I know,' I said. I handed him the shovel I had been using.

'What's this for?'

'How else are we going to get him out?'

'We were never going to sell out, remember?' Justin said. He took the shovel and struck the laundry wall. At first nothing happened. The elephant shuddered. But with the second strike the wallpaper started to tear, and the plaster wall showed through. Soon we saw what was inside, jib and cheap wood, easy to tear down.

'I'm so happy you came back,' I whispered.

I took up the ironing board and struck the wall. Then the elephant was moving, pushing at the structure, his head breaking wood. Justin hit the wall again and again, his arms making great arcs, dust flying, until the elephant could walk through.

We carried the children out and put them in the trailer. The elephant gestured with his trunk, and we began.

When my mother-in-law arrived she would find the house empty, with a great hole in the wall of the laundry, and the dishes left unwashed on the bench.

Katriona went on ahead, black hair moving in the light. She would contact people all along the way, a network of escapees.

Massive species loss. Imminent climate change. All going to fall apart. My head is screwed on. I'm organising my way out.

I touched the elephant's side, stroked his map of skin. He knew where we were going. To roam, to meander, to bury our dead, to remember.

Previous Publications

'The Beauty of Mrs Lim' won the Sunday Star Times Short Story Award, and was published in that paper in 2017

'The Apologia' appeared in *Headland Issue Four*

'The Free Box' was published in *Best New Zealand Fiction Volume Four,* Random House

'The Conservation of the Stars' was published in *Westerly 61.1*, by guest editor Stephan Kinnane who is a Marda Marda from Mirrawong country in the East Kimberly

Acknowledgements

Michalia Arathimos is winner of the 2020 Carmel Bird Digital Literary Award for *Apologia*. The judge of the 2020 award was Justin Wolfers.

This award is named in honour of renowned Australian author Carmel Bird, who has published a range of short fiction, novels and books on writing and was awarded the Patrick White Award for Literature in 2016.

Launched in 2017, the Carmel Bird Digital Literary Award is an annual competition that showcases new works of short fiction up to 30,000 words in length from Australian writers. It is run by Spineless Wonders and supported by the Copyright Agency's Cultural Fund.

Finalists in the Carmel Bird Digital Literary Award are published electronically by Spineless Wonders.

www.shortaustralianstories.com.au

Biography

Michalia Arathimos is a Greek writer. She has published work in *The Lifted Brow*, *Westerly*, *Overland*, *Landfall* and elsewhere, and is *Overland*'s fiction reviewer. Her novel, *Aukati*, was published by Mākaro Press. She is the Writer in Residence at Randell Cottage and will hold the Grimshaw Sargeson Fellowship in 2021.

About This Series

Apologia by Michalia Arathimos is published as part of the Spineless Wonders Smalls series of small format paperbacks released to celebrate our tenth year in publishing.

To find out about other books published in this series, go to www.shortaustralianstories.com.au

www.shortaustralianstories.com.au

www.ingramcontent.com/pod-product-compliance
Lightning Source LLC
Chambersburg PA
CBHW030802190726
48285CB00003B/978